CAT'S NIGHT OUT

TALES FROM THE FEDERAL WITCH

T S PAUL

GREAT GOD PAN PUBLISHING

Special thanks to my wife Heather who keeps me grounded and to Merlin the Cat, we are his minions.

GRANDMOTHER BLACKMORE

T S PAUL

This story takes place after Agatha's seventh birthday party and the collapse of her mother.

"I can't take her. Look what happened to her own mother! No. I won't put my own family at risk."

"Camilla, she is your family. Don't you understand?"

"No means no, Mother. She is too dangerous. You take her."

I stood back and stared at my daughter. "Fine. I will take her and raise her as my own. She is family, after all."

Camilla looked at me with a frown on her face and turned away. It was all I could do to just shake my head at her. Her own sister's child. Speaking of the child...I looked around and spotted young Agatha sitting on the porch. She was talking to something on the table.

"Make me bigger again!"

"I can't. I don't know the spell. I tried to fix you once and you shrank, remember?"

The tiny unicorn paced the table in front of the small Witch child. "I hate being small. Change me back! Please?"

"Agatha, dear?" She looked up at my voice with sad eyes. "Who is your friend?"

"I'm not sure what his name is. He doesn't like me." Agatha peered down at the small unicorn.

I gave the male Unicorn a look. "Well? Do you have a name?"

"Who the hell are you? Of course, I have a name. My name is Fergus."

"Well Fergus, my name is Marcella Blackmore, and this is my granddaughter Agatha. What are we to do with you? Hmmm?"

"You look like a big shot Witch. Change me back! Make me big again!" Fergus stomped his feet on the table and marched around in a circle.

"You are the first talking Unicorn I have ever met, and I have met a few. Let me explain something about Witches and spells. Small cantrips or household spells can be performed by any Witch. Those are well known and reversible. Original or larger spells are almost impossible to reverse. Only the Witch that laid the spell can remove it. Especially those that are cast instinctively. If I tried, bad things might happen, such as you being turned into a cabbage."

"So I'm stuck like this? Crap! This is why my people hate Witches and humans. Always screwing around with the natural order of things. I'm hungry. Got any hay around?"

"Agatha, why don't you take Fergus into the house and show him the guest room you like the best?"

"OK, Grandmother." She scooped the protesting Unicorn up and ran into the house. I watched her go and sighed. I sat in the chair Agatha had vacated and grabbed the phone from the table.

Dialing the number from memory, I called Cappy first. "Cappy, this is Marcella Blackmore."

"Yes, Mrs. Blackmore."

"I have my granddaughter Agatha here at the house with me. She is going to live here, in case anyone asks."

"Is that the same girl who shrank the Unicorn the other day?"

"It is. Camilla refuses to take her, and no granddaughter of mine will go to humans to raise. She stays with family."

"Yes, Ma'am. I will spread the word if anyone asks. I'm sure you can control her Magick."

"That is correct, Cappy. Thank you for your time." I hung up and stared at the phone. Cappy was like the town crier. He would spread any sort of gossip all over the county. Better than a newspaper.

"Is he coming here for me? Did mommy die?" I looked down to see little Agatha at my feet, with tears in her eyes. Quickly I went down on my knees.

"No, dear. Your mother is just sick. Nothing's your fault."

"But, but, Auntie Camilla said...she said it was all my fault!" The dam of tears broke free, and the little girl began to sob.

By all that is holy, I should eject that girl from the coven! 'Camilla, what did you do?' Inside I was fuming. Glancing to the left, I watched as the candle display near the door began to melt on its own. I tried to reign in both my anger and my power.

Taking a deep breath, I let it out slowly and smiled at Agatha. "Little one, none of this is your fault. You are a Witch from a long line of Witches. Our ancestors defeated evil the likes of which would scare people like your Aunt. Witches are expected to do great magic, and those of our line are some of the greatest. Ignore her."

Agatha gave me a big hug which almost brought me to tears myself. Neither of my own daughters hugs me anymore.

I brushed the silky black strands of hair out of her face and kissed her forehead. "Dry those tears, young lady. We have a great many things to do today that don't require tears. Where did you leave Fergus?"

"I put him in the dollhouse. He's mean! What did I do to him that was wrong?" The tears started to come out again.

Taking my fingers, I wiped them away and gave her a smile. "He's just upset. Like you, he had a shock today. Come along and let's see what he's up to. There are lots of breakable things in this house."

I stood and took Agatha's hand. The stairs were a bit too steep for a child this small. "Wait here a moment, dear." I said a small prayer to my Goddess and spoke a word of power.

"Whee! Grandmother, I'm flying!" The young girl levitated up to the second-floor landing.

I had to smile. My own girls loved that the most. I grew sad thinking of them. I forced a smile for the young girl. "Did you like that?"

"I did! Let's do it again!"

Chuckling at her enthusiasm, I scooped her up and held her in my arms. "We will another time. I promise! Now, which room did you go to?"

Agatha led me down the hall to the room at the end. The door was already ajar, and we could both hear a growl. Oh, no! Zeus! I jerked the door open and stopped just inside the room.

Zeus was a Savannah Cat, specially bred to be trainable like a dog and much bigger than the average house cat. Much bigger. He was on his hind legs, paws flat on the dresser, growling at the mini-Unicorn who was perched on the very top of my mother's antique mirror.

"Zeus! Down!" The cat gave Fergus a final growl and put his feet on the ground. We both received a glare as he swished his way out of the room, tail in the air.

"Grandmother, your cat is huge! Does he bite?" Agatha's eyes were wide open.

"He only bites Camilla, so you are safe, dear one."

I turned to stare at the Unicorn. "By the Gods, how did you get up there?"

"I jumped! Nobody said anything about Lions being loose in the house! Change me back!"

Unicorns. I shook my head 'no' as I reached up for him. "I told you, Fergus. That is almost impossible for me to do and not harm you. However, I will make you a deal."

The Unicorn stepped into my hand and looked up at me. "What sort of deal?"

"If you behave and stay here with us I will send for the best magical detectives in the business. I will do everything in my power to find help for you. Do we have a deal?"

"I have to stay here? With that Lion out there? No deal!" The small Unicorn nipped my finger, so I dropped him.

"Aieee!" He screamed as he fell about five feet to the floor where he bounced like a ball and rolled under the dresser.

"Why the freaking hell did you do that? Can't you see I'm breakable? Crazy ass witches."

"Fergus." Silence.

"Fergus! Come out here right now." I bent down to look under the dresser.

"No! You tried to kill me!"

"Are you dead?"

"No..."

"Do you have broken bones or any injuries at all?"

"No. What did you do to me? Is this some kind of trick?"

I waved the Unicorn closer. "Fergus, when animals are affected by magic they can change in many ways. One of these is they become immune to magic and are indestructible. You can still die from disease or old age, but you cannot be harmed externally. Do you understand what I mean by that?"

"What do I look like, a donkey? My parents educated me, thank you very much! I know what that means. Duh. So the cat can't eat me?"

"Well, he can still swallow you, but chewing isn't possible. Don't let him do any of that. It might hurt him."

"Hurt him?" The Unicorn shuddered. "That might scare me half to death!"

I grabbed him and set him on top of the bed. "So how did you really get all the way up there?" I pointed to the mirror.

"Already told you. I jumped. Do you have any hay around here?"

5

He began to trot back and forth across the bed, much to Agatha's delight.

"There may be some out in the garden. I will round up something for you later."

"Did you put Fergus in the dollhouse?" I pointed toward the family heirloom.

"Yes, Grandmother. Did he damage it?"

"It doesn't look like it. This was once your great-great-great-great-great Grandmother's room. The dollhouse belonged to her. Many of the things in this room were hers. Would you like this to be your new room?" My gaze fixated upon a small box on the dresser. For just a split second it gleamed at me.

"Can it? Oh, Grandmother! It's beautiful." She scooped up Fergus. "Isn't it beautiful, Fergus?"

"Yeah, kid. Beautiful. Not a single strand of hay in sight."

I glanced back at the box and opened it. A dusty bag lay in the center. I must have been imagining things, I thought to myself as I closed the box. I moved it off the dresser and placed it in the curio cabinet near the door. I was snapping the lock closed as Agatha came over.

"Grandmother, what's in there?" She pointed.

"That holds some family heirlooms that belonged to my Grandmother. One day I will show you. But not today, OK?" She nodded at me but continued to stare.

"Good. Let's go find some food for the starving beast, shall we?"

Fergus stopped running and froze. "Beast? Where?"

Agatha giggled. "She means you, dummy!"

She scooped him up just as he said, "Oh."

The stairs were easier to go down than up for Agatha. I saved my power for more important things. Still smiling, I led the both of them through the house to the garden outside.

"I have very few rules in my house, but this is a big one. Never go into the Garden alone. This is the oldest Witch's garden on this side of the world. It has been here ever since we came to this country with

Sir Walter Raleigh in 1585. Our ancestors were here first before any of our brethren. Later, when this town was first founded, our ancestors allowed it to happen and helped the colonists to establish themselves. There is ancient magick here, child. Respect it."

"Yes, Grandmother. I will." She looked around at the flowers and herbs.

"Fergus. What did you eat?"

I looked at Agatha but couldn't see the Unicorn. Scanning the garden, I spotted the little devil eating my prized zinnias!

"Stop! Those are not food!"

Chewing a mouthful of flowers, the Unicorn froze. "Mmmmph?"

"Yes, you. Stop eating my flowers or being small is the least of your worries!"

The Unicorn spat out the flowers and started to apologize. I waved him off. "I have a collection of grasses over here. You may graze 'til your heart's content on two conditions. Never eat all of one kind and leave my flowers alone. Got it?"

He nodded.

"Good. Let me show you. Agatha, these are all cooking herbs here in this part of the garden. Nothing here in this small section can hurt you." I pointed to the small garden gate's sign that said, "kitchen herbs." A thatched fence bordered the area, complete with a picnic table and play area.

"There is your grass, Fergus." I pointed to the play area.

I lowered myself to my knees. "This is the only part of the garden you are allowed, for now. It is completely safe for the both of you. Understand?" Agatha nodded.

"Wonderful. As you get older, I will introduce you to the rest of it."

I spent the rest of the afternoon teaching her the names of the herbs and telling her their uses. She and Fergus were tired out by the end of the day.

After I had put her to bed, I watched her sleep. Fergus was curled up on a pillow next to her. I spoke to my daughter Teegan. "She is unique, Teegan. Your daughter will be a marvel when she grows up." I sent prayers of healing toward the hospital where my daughter resided. The reason for her illness was fatigue and heartbreak. Her husband had been her entire life, and now he was gone. I blew out a breath. What was I going to do with a seven-year-old around here?

A flash of light startled me out of my thoughts. I turned and looked behind me. The curio cabinet was glowing!

With wide eyes, I removed my Grandmother's enforcer bracelet from the bag it had resided in for over twenty-five years. It was glowing.

I closed the cabinet and removed myself to my study downstairs. The bracelet had never glowed for a member of the family in living memory.

What am I to do with you now? I stared at the now dull bracelet. It had never reacted to me, so it had to be Agatha. Did it mean that she was destined to be an enforcer, or did it mean something else? I needed a seer, and I needed one as soon as possible.

I LOOKED at the boxes stacked in the foyer and smiled. This year was going to be special. I could remember the good years with my husband and the girls playing and dancing beneath the tree. A small tear rolled down my cheek. I shook my head and wiped my face. Those days were long gone. But I had a new voice and breath of freshness in the house now. I needed to move forward and start living for the future again. So much to do, so little time. It was time to call in the coven and put them to work.

"Grandma, are we moving?" I looked down, and Agatha stood at my feet.

Reaching down, I brushed her hair from her eyes. "No, little one. It will be Yule soon, and these boxes contain all the decorations. Do you want to help put them up?"

My little granddaughter has the biggest smile, and she graced me with it. "Yes, please."

I stepped over to the largest box and started to pull out several clear plastic cases filled with ornaments. "Sometime today, Cappy will join us. He went over to the Three Sisters Farm to pick out a tree for us. I told him that the Sanderson sisters always keep a nice one back for me. When we get it set up, you and Fergus can help me decorate. Does that sound good to you?"

"Can I? Momma never lets me help. Daddy...Daddy told me that when I was older, I could help."

"You miss them, don't you, dear?"

Agatha sniffed. "I miss my mommy."

Giving her a big hug, I squeezed her to me. "Honey, we can go see her if you like. She's not too far away."

"OK. Is Auntie Camilla going to be there, too?"

"Do you want her to be?"

Agatha put her head back down and hid her face. A muffled "No," could be heard. It was all I could do not to curse my daughter's name. She had terrified this little one so much.

I held her away from my body so I could see her face. "The coven is coming this afternoon to decorate. I want you to help. Afterward, we can talk about going to see Teegan, your mommy. Does that suit you, dear?"

She nodded her head.

"Good. Now where did you leave that rascal of a Unicorn?"

———

"TALLY HO!" Fergus put his head down and charged his attacker. The field mouse riding the crow dodged him and tried to stab him with its lance.

Dancing to one side Fergus yelled, "You missed me!"

He had been eating some choice hay in the garden and watching out for hawks, when suddenly he was attacked by a mouse dressed in armor and riding a large crow.

"What's with the black chicken? Trying to cross the road?"

The crow cocked its head at the mini-Unicorn, and its shiny black eye gleamed with intelligence in the light of the sun. The mouse knight readjusted its lance and tapped the crow. The two of them launched into the sky.

"Can't take a joke, can ya! Good riddance." Fergus watched them fly off into the sky, and he snorted. The hay patch was looking mighty fine at the moment.

Unknown to Fergus, the diminutive knight and his steed didn't leave, but looped around and were lining up for the kill. The shadow of the crow was like an arrow from the gods as it raced across the garden aimed straight at Fergus's heart.

THUNDER ROLLED, and there was a flash of light. The mouse warrior and his mount were frozen in the air.

"Shoo! Shoo!" I raised my hands to release the pair, waving the crow and its rider away. "You know the rules. The Unicorn is under my protection. Stay in your own territory. Tell your King I will be watching in the future."

Looking down, I could see Fergus cowering behind my shoes. "You can come out now."

"What the flaming hell was that!"

"That was one of the mice-knights. I believe I told you to stay away from the mice?" I gave the small Unicorn my sternest look.

"Uh, I may have heard you say that. But why was a mouse riding a crow?" Fergus allowed Agatha to pick him up.

I sighed. Time for a history lesson. "Agatha, bring Fergus over to the table." We sat down at the picnic table, and Fergus explored the table top.

"When our ancestors explored and settled in this area, they first created the Garden. I have told you about how it is the oldest Witch Garden this side of Europe. Entire generations of our family have worked magic on the land here. This Garden has been the focal point for it all. Magic changes things, especially living creatures. Both Fergus and the squirrels are good examples of this. As Witches, we try very hard to not work magic upon live creatures. They take on magical aspects, the most common of which is magical immunity."

I caught Agatha's eye. "The mice were already living in the area when the Garden was created. They have changed over the years. Out there, is a mouse kingdom of intelligent mice that are immune to magic. We made a bargain with them years ago that they would keep to the Garden and not cause trouble. However, their new King has been pushing the boundaries of our deal. Hence the crows. Try to avoid them if possible. Magic cannot hurt them, and they are not afraid of us. Do you understand?"

"Grandmother, do they have houses and things?"

"Agatha, honey, I have no idea. My mother always told me to respect the bargain and stay away from them. They live in that direction." I pointed toward the north part of the Garden.

"I almost got that one, but he ran away! The horn is all-powerful!" Fergus shook his head and horn and pranced about.

"Come along, little warrior. The coven should be here soon, and we have a house to decorate." I led the two of them back toward the house.

I could see movement ahead as we approached the huge Victorian style house we lived in. Coven members were draping fresh pine boughs across the porch and window eaves. Cappy's truck was just pulling up, so the Sanderson sisters must have come through with a fabulous tree.

"Agatha, child. Why don't you go get cleaned up? When you come down you may join us in decorating."

I watched as she ran up the back steps and into the kitchen. Smiling, I approached Cappy as he stared into the back of his truck.

He gave me a short bow and addressed me as 'Milady.'

I smiled but gave him a stern look. "Cappy, you do not have to do that outside of the covenstead."

"I am aware of that Milady, but it suits me to do it. Now. Those sisters have outdone themselves this year. This has to be the biggest tree we have ever had. I'm not entirely sure how we got it into the truck." The tree in question was a Norwegian Spruce that simply filled the back of his truck. It was eight feet tall, and as he said, the largest in years. I took it as a good omen for the coming year.

It was well that Agatha was not underfoot as we muscled the tree into the house. Half of those attending to the decorations were needed to just get it through the front door. It was marvelous and looked as if it had grown in place in the living room. It was going to be an eventful celebration.

The murmured voices of those helping to decorate could barely be heard when Agatha reappeared. She was dressed as a princess and was very cute.

"Is this our tree?"

"It is, dear one. Do you like it?"

I watched as she circled the tree, stepping close to the wall to get all the way around. "He says you have turned his best side to the light."

I felt my eyebrows go up. "Who says that, Agatha? Did you bring Fergus down with you?"

"No, he's watching TV upstairs. I was talking about Boamire. He likes the potion you put into the stand." She continued to stroke the branches of the tree and circle it. Could she really be talking to the tree? There was a spell I could use to converse with the plants, but even I have never spoken to a Yule tree.

"Would you like to help me decorate Boamire? We have a great many things to place upon him."

Agatha smiled at me but continued to stare at the tree.

Opening the first box, I began to pull out hand-knitted lace garland and my grandmother's tree skirt. Many of my decorations had been in the family for a century or more. I said a word of power and caused the garland to circle the tree, only helping it along near the bottom.

With Agatha helping, the decorations went up far faster than in more recent years. "What about the top, Grandmother?"

"That, Agatha, is for you to help with. We have a selection. You must pick the one for this year, and I will lift you up to place it." I pointed to the five symbols arrayed on the floor. Each represented an element: Earth, Air, Fire, Water, Spirit.

"This one!" She held up a gold and silver pine cone from one of the majestic Redwoods of far off California. It symbolized Earth.

"Excellent! Now hold on." I spoke a word of power and lifted her up. She squealed happily as she took flight. Carefully, she placed the cone at the top of the tree.

Setting her back down, I smiled at her. "Now, we have cooking to do for tonight. Do you wish to help, or would you like to go play with Fergus?"

"Can I sit here and talk to Boamire?"

"Of course you can, dear. Call me if you need anything." I watched as she grabbed a pillow off the couch and sat in front of the tree. Every so often she would say something as if she were carrying on a conversation with the tree.

THE WINTER SOLSTICE Yule celebration was a major gathering here at the house. Our entire valley was protected from harm by generations of magic users. The house was the focal point for the magic, and it was its presence that prevented winter storms from ravaging the valley. So far this winter, we had been spared the snow. This was a season for feasting, drinking and for sacrifice. This was the pinnacle of the eternal battle between the Oak King and the Holly King. It was the passing of the seasons. We would celebrate the changing of the seasons and toast to the King's victory over his brother.

As I dressed for the celebration, I could hear the guests arrive. It was traditional for me to dress as my ancestors did. I favored the more formal outfits from a century ago, but this year I chose that of the first Blackmore.

Standing at the top of the stairs, I watched my friends and family gather in the foyer. The house would only be opened after I made my formal entrance. I cleared my throat and made my grand entrance to the party. For this occasion, I wore a houppelande over my party dress. The outer robe is similar to that of academic robes used in colleges. Mine was decorated with gems and gold thread, depicting our history and our future as Witches.

"Greetings one and all and welcome to our annual gathering of the Briarwood Coven. Merry meet and Merry part and Merry meet again. Welcome, all of you, to my home." I descended the stairs and clasped hands with many old friends along the way.

"You always have to make the grand entrance. How are you, mother?" Camilla clasped my hand but refused a hug.

"I am fine. Are you here alone or did you bring Harrison and the girls?"

Camilla frowned at me and made an ugly face. "His name is Harvey. You know very well that Harrison died last year. The girls went to church with Harvey. His family has a large to-do. Besides, they have chosen their own path. Is Agatha here?"

"Of course she is. She and Fergus should be around here somewhere. She is family, after all."

"Fergus, who is Fergus?" Camilla looked around the room at all the visitors.

She didn't know. I smiled at that. "Fergus is the name of the Unicorn. He is quite frisky for one so young."

"The Unicorn? Mother, talking to Unicorns, at your age?"

"You leave my age out of this conversation, young lady. I am still your mother, and don't you forget it. Now, go circulate please." I shook my head, wondering why she even bothers anymore.

Many of my oldest friends were here, as well as some I didn't know. I wandered the room, greeting new faces and old. It was at the back of the room that I found the woman I searched for.

"Kassandra, thank you for coming." I embraced the much older woman sitting in one of my overstuffed chairs in front of the fire.

"Milady Blackmore, I would not have missed it for the world." Kassandra was at least eighty years old and was the oldest seer on the continent.

"Did you get my message about Verity's bracelet?"

"I did. In fact, I have been watching your granddaughter since I arrived." She pointed.

Looking in the direction her finger pointed, I saw Agatha still dressed in the princess outfit, sitting out of the way in front of the tree.

"She claims it's talking to her."

Kassandra looked up at me. "It is. If you listen very carefully, you can catch a phrase here and there. Where did you get this one?"

"The Sanderson sisters. They claimed it grew just for me."

"They might be right. Or rather it was grown just for her. Has she done anything else to shock the neighbors?"

"Not yet. By the Gods, Kassandra, neither of my daughters had a third of the power she exudes. I'm not sure I can train a Witch such as she."

Kassandra reached up to take my hand. "Marcella, she will become the best of us. Under her leadership, our coven will accomplish great things. She is the linchpin that will make or break relations with the humans. Empires will rise, and empires will fall. But all will bow to the Maker, the Taker, the Giver, and the Breaker. She will tame the beasts and rise to the heavens. Even the Gods will know their own. Doom be to those who cross her, but love will conquer the world." Kassandra sagged in her seat and looked up at me again.

"Did I just make a prophecy?"

"You did. I will teach her everything I know." I repeated the prophecy to her.

"Do that," she said. "Even the Gods..."

I felt the world shift.

The house gave a slight shiver and then a rumble. Everyone in the house froze and then burst into conversation. Earthquakes in Maine were extremely rare. I turned to speak to Kassandra when again when everything went sideways!

The house shook, and a loud crack sounded through the house. Many of the party goers were thrown to the floor. Cries of "Earthquake!" sounded through the house.

I felt a surge of magic that made my ears ring, and then the house settled back down.

"What...What was that?" I asked.

Kassandra didn't answer me but was staring at Agatha with wide eyes.

The little girl got up from where she was sitting and approached me. "Grandmother, I fixed Boamire. He doesn't hurt anymore!"

"You did? What did you do?" I suddenly realized that she was the cause of the earthquake.

"I gave him his roots back." She smiled at me with the cutest dimples on her face.

Glancing at the Yule tree, I noticed that it no longer sat in the special tree stand. It now grew out of the very floor. "Agatha, dear. Does the tree grow through the floor now?"

"Of course not. That would be silly, Grandmother. Bugs and things could come through the hole. This is better. He's now part of the house. Forever! Now I can always talk to him and hear his stories." She skipped back and sat down next to the tree.

Kassandra looked over at me and spoke a quote I barely remembered. "For I am the Soul of Nature, who giveth life to the universe..."

My house now had a tree growing out of it?

———

I LAID my head down on my desk and felt a tear roll down my cheek. It was very hard to hate your own child, but I was getting there with Camilla. By the Gods, why did she have to make this so hard?

Looking at my personal altar next to my desk, I said a tiny prayer and mentioned that my question was rhetorical. You never know with the Gods.

In front of me on the desk was a long list of schools with red Xs next to each name. My own daughter had managed to sabotage any attempt on my part to enroll Agatha anywhere for elementary school. Raising my head up, I gently placed both hands on my forehead and concentrated on my Third-Eye Chakra. Wisdom and intuition were enhanced by this part of the brain. My choices were simple. Send the poor child away to boarding school or teach her myself. I suspected that Camilla wished for me to send her away. The simple fact of doing that would hobble her as a Witch. Overseas boarding schools weren't like those in the Wizarding books. I needed to find out how I could teach her and not run afoul of the educational authorities.

Wiping my eyes, I sat up straight, picked up the phone and dialed. "Harry, I need to understand how Maine treats homeschooling. Can you check into that for me?"

Harry was one of my oldest friends and one of the best lawyers in the state. He could answer any question for me.

I listened for a moment and answered the questions he asked me. "That's fine, then. It's Camilla again. She took it upon herself to block Agatha from all the schools within any reasonable driving distance. I will have to teach her myself, then. I want to be able to do so legally and without issues."

Harry's calm voice at the other end of the line told me everything that I wanted to hear. We set up an appointment for later that afternoon to go over his firm's findings.

"Agatha? Are you here?" I called up the stairs. Not hearing anything, I went outside onto the porch. She had so far kept to the rules and not strayed into the Garden alone.

I heard the giggling and laughing the moment I stepped outside. Agatha and Zeus were roughhousing out on the lawn. Even though

Zeus was a very large cat, he acted like a dog. Agatha would throw one of his toys. Zeus would catch it and then they would chase each other to get the toy back. It looked like a fun game!

"Agatha, dear!" The little girl paused in her pursuit of the cat and ran instead toward me.

"Yes, Grandmother?" Her clothes were a mess, covered in grass stains and leaves but she had the biggest smile on her face.

"We are going to go into town for a couple of errands. Can you go and get changed?"

"I can! Can we get ice cream?" Agatha ran toward me and gave me a big hug.

"Of course we can. Where is Fergus?"

"He's upstairs watching TV. Do you want me to bring him along?"

"Please do. Now run along. We have an appointment with a friend of mine in a couple of hours, so scoot." I watched Aggie run into the house.

"Meow." I looked down at my familiar.

"Happy? I know she's a handful, but I appreciate you helping." Sometimes I wondered how my conversations with Zeus appeared to others. Crazy cat lady, some might say. Zeus was a gift from a friend. A re-gift, if you must know. Too much cat for them. His breed made him one of the largest domesticated house cats on the planet. In some ways, he was smarter than some of the townspeople around here. He was certainly more attractive than most of them.

Zeus meowed at me and rubbed up against my legs. I didn't have to reach far to scratch his head. "I know buddy, I know. Go play. Try not to eat Fergus when you play with him."

I stepped into the house and climbed the stairs to my room. Unlike Agatha's, mine was at the very end of the hall. It was traditionally the head of the clan's room. It had secrets of its own and guarded them well. Selecting business casual clothing, I quickly changed and went to check up on Agatha.

I could hear her speaking to Fergus as I approached the door.

"...I really want to go. Please?"

"He's here all by himself all day long. Fergus, Zeus just wants to play."

"That's not 'play.' He wants to eat me! I see the way he looks at me with those beady cat eyes. Please, don't leave me alone."

Knocking on the door, I stepped inside. "Agatha, are you ready to go?"

She was sitting in front of my grandmother's antique dollhouse. Fergus was perched upon one of the toy beds. "Hi, Grandmother. Fergus wants to come with us."

I looked down at the miniature Unicorn and smiled. "He's your familiar now, dear. You should take him everywhere with you. I will show you how to store your power inside of him."

"Wait? She's going to do what to me?" Fergus hopped out of the dollhouse onto Agatha's outstretched hand.

"Store power. I will explain it all to you later, Fergus." I took Agatha's hand as she stood up.

"Now, you need a place for Fergus to stay close to you." I scrutinized my granddaughter's outfit.

Pointing, I showed her the perfect spot. "See if he will fit in your shirt pocket. I can have your shirts modified, so his horn and hooves don't destroy the fabric."

Agatha slipped the now protesting Unicorn into her shirt pocket. "See? He fits perfectly."

We both could hear the Unicorn mumbling and trying to speak inside the pocket. "Fergus, that is a perfect place for you, and you know it. Less chance of a hawk or a cat getting a hold on you." The struggling Unicorn settled down immediately. I winked at Agatha.

"Now, we have to stop first at Harry's, my lawyer's office, and then we can get you some ice cream as well as some new clothes. Does that sound good to you?"

"I get a choice?" Agatha had wide eyes.

"Of course, dear. It is your life. I only want the very best for you."

She gave me a big hug. "I'm good."

I laughed and held her hand as we went down the stairs. I seldom drove, but I did know how. My 1971 Land Rover sat in the garage next to Teegan's old station wagon. According to Camilla, there was no room at her house for it. A member of the coven had placed it up on blocks and took care of servicing it for me. Getting it back in service was way easier that way.

"Is this your car? Why is the steering wheel on this side?" Agatha was full of questions as she climbed inside.

"This was a gift from a very old friend. It's a British car, so the wheel is different. They drive on the opposite side of the road over there."

"They do? Why?"

"That is an excellent question, Agatha. It's like this. During the ancient times, most people carried swords when they traveled. They expected an attack from the right as most of the world is right-handed. So people walked or rode on the left to prepare for this. When cars were invented, they continued to use the left side."

Agatha scrunched up her face and stared at me. "That doesn't make sense, Grandmother. If they drive like that why doesn't everyone else? Wasn't America founded by the British?"

Inwardly, I cheered. Power and intelligence. I could teach her so much! "It's France's fault. During the French Revolution, a man named Napoleon decided that his troops should travel on the right to be different from the rest of the world. When cars were invented, they stayed that way. Here in this country, we were torn, and both ways were used for years until finally, the government decreed that we would drive on the right side of the road."

Many of the local cars I passed slowed when they caught sight of my Land Rover. Most everyone in town knew my car, even though I drove infrequently. My lawyer's office was in the center of town near the courthouse. Carefully, I parked in front and got out.

"Come along, Agatha." I opened the car door and took her hand.

"Who is Fielding, Stone, and Sullivan?" She pointed to the sign out in front of the building.

"Those are the lawyers who work here. My friend Harry Stone is the one we are meeting." I led her up the stairs and into the building.

"Good afternoon, Mrs. Blackmore." Roz, the receptionist, called my name.

"Hello, Rosalind. How are your children?" She blushed that I remembered.

"Well, Nostradamus just finished the police academy and already has a job lined up with Cappy. The girls are starting high school next year."

"Tell Bull that I look forward to having him up at the house for dinner sometime. He earned it, after all the work he did around the place last year. He's a good boy." I forgot and used his nickname rather than his real name. Roz preferred his given name to be used.

"This is Agatha, my granddaughter. We are here to see Harry." Roz smiled but gave Agatha a hard stare. Pressing a button, she called Harry.

"Come along dear. It's this way." Harry's office was at the end of the hall. He might not get top billing, but he was the one with the most experience, having once been a judge.

I knocked, but Harry yelled anyway. "Marcella, get in here."

Harry looked much the same as the last time I saw him. Skinny as a rail and bald as a stone. He politely shook Agatha's hand and pointed her toward a chair.

Always to the point, he didn't waste time. "I looked up what you asked about. Maine law states that she must be in school at least 175 days out of every year. A basic curriculum must be followed as well as computer science. The local school board must be notified, but since they refused to admit her, they can't complain about it too much."

"Can we sue the school board about the denial of education?" I saw Harry wince.

"We can, but I don't advise it. Marcella, your daughter Camilla did a real number on this innocent child here. She convinced the board, as well as half the private schools in the state, that Agatha is dangerous and that she is the reason Teegan is hospitalized." Harry held out a pack of paper to me.

Skimming the stack, I could see statements from schools and headmasters. I had only asked Harry to look into my problem that morning. He was fast.

"So can I do it?"

"Of course you can. Homeschooling is very easy. There are lesson plans available from the internet. You can get tutors for the subjects that you can't do."

"Thank you, Harry. This is a big help." I smiled at my old friend.

"Anything for you Marcella, you know that. Now, I have one more bit of business." He handed me a document.

"I prepared this, in the off-chance Camilla starts more trouble. This gives you Power of Attorney over Agatha so that for all intents and purposes she is now your daughter. Legally, you will adopt her."

I stared in shock at the document in my hand. Teegan's signature was at the top, as well as her departed husband's. It only lacked mine.

"How? How did you get this, Harry?"

"Your daughter and her husband set it up. She didn't trust her sister to follow any of her instructions, so this was prepared. The problem was, it was done the week before Michael's death, and in all the confusion, Teegan forgot to tell me to have you sign it."

I nodded, remembering the chaos of that time. I grabbed a pen and scribbled my name in the empty box. "There. Does this mean she's mine?"

"Once the court says so. But yes. I have a favor or two I can pull, and I will take care of it. Don't worry. Camilla is now unable to pull anything."

"Thank you again, Harry. If there is anything I can do, just let me know." I stood and took Agatha's hand.

"Just pay my bill, and all will be right with my world and Dan's. You know how he gets if people don't pay. Nice meeting you Miss Blackmore. I will expect great things from you." He took Agatha's hand and shook it.

We said goodbye to Roz and stepped out of the building right into Camilla!

"Mother! How dare you bring that walking time bomb into this town! She could spell us all into pink chickens!"

"'She' has a name. Her magic isn't dangerous, despite all the trouble you, yourself, have caused her. Really Camilla, preventing the child from even going to school. That is low even for you."

My daughter's face changed from outrage to fury. "What is that supposed to mean? She is a threat to my children, and I won't have it. Send her away to some boarding school somewhere."

"I think not. She is going to be taught right here in Briarwood." I smiled at her.

"Over my dead body, she will. I have already spoken to both the school board and the state board about..." She froze when she realized what she had admitted.

"That is what I just learned. Nice of you to admit it. No, she is going to be homeschooled by me. So suck it up, buttercup." I muttered a spell under my breath and said "Begone!" Camilla was dragged from my sight by a sudden magnetic force.

"Is she gone?" Agatha came out from behind the bushes in front of Harry's office.

"She is, little one. My spell only dragged her to the hair salon, but it should cause a bit of gossip, nonetheless. Let's go get that ice cream." We piled back into my Land Rover and went to the opposite edge of town.

The ice cream parlor was next to one of the town's little parks. Patrons could sit and eat their ice cream at tables by the park's edge. Purple squirrels leapt from trees and played in the park by the dozens. They were the result of an accidental release of magic by Agatha when she was four.

"Grandmother! My squirrels. It's my squirrels!" Agatha pulled out of my hand and ran to the nearest table in the park.

I sat next to her as she tried to feed one of the squirrels some ice cream. "Do you remember them?"

Agatha looked so much like Teegan for a moment. "I do. Mommy used to bring me here. The squirrels like me."

"You can play with them, but keep me in sight, OK?" She nodded and ran to play near the trees. I could see her showing Fergus the purple tree rats.

I looked up at the sky. By the gods! I was a mother all over again. Could I do it? Watching the little brunette run around made me smile. I would teach her. She was destined to change the world, and I would help her to the best of my ability. I glanced back and was shocked. It was as if she were holding court. Over twenty squirrels surrounded her now, and were listening to every word she said. I stood and walked over near her.

"...Mommy's sick and nasty Auntie Camilla gave me to Grandmother. I have more magic now. Look at Fergus." She pointed to the mini-Unicorn.

"Agatha, is everything alright?" The squirrels all cleared out just as fast as their little purple tails could carry them.

"Of course, Grandmother. I was just talking to my friends."

"Oh. Well, it's time to go home. We have much to plan for your schooling." I took her hand and led her back to the car. Looking back, I could see that her friends had gathered back together on the grass. Those rodents have never been the same since she zapped them.

We had a grand future to plan, and I couldn't wait to start. I would have to call in a few favors, but Agatha would get the best education I could provide for her. She was going to do great things, and I wanted to see it.

Behind me, the squirrels gathered and made plans of their own.

CAMILLA'S OBSESSION

T S PAUL

This story takes place when Camilla and Teegan Blackmore were teenagers.

"Look Cammie, Unicorns!" Teegan pointed to the field across the road.

"Nice. Did you see the library here?"

"Is that all you care about, Cam? Libraries? What sort of fun is that? Relax a little." Camilla's younger sister frowned at her.

"My name is Camilla. Not Cam. Not Milla. And especially not Cammie. It's Camilla."

Teegan made a face pantomiming her sister. "I know, I know. Camilla. Like I haven't heard it my whole friggin' life. Mom brought us here to have fun, not to stare at books all day."

Camilla turned to her sister. "Books are important. As heir, I have to know things. How to run a coven, conduct a circle, spellwork. Stuff like that."

"Mom's never said which of us was the heir. You know that! One of the elders told me it was flexible."

Camilla waved. "Those old biddies? They just say stuff to confuse us. I've tried talking to them before."

"Some of those ladies are my friends. Do you have to be mean all the time?"

"I'm not mean!" Camilla protested.

"The question was rhetorical, anyway." Teegan stepped off the porch and ran for the fence containing the Unicorns.

"Idiot. She will never understand." Camilla barely acknowledged that her sister had left. 'Hereditary Witches and their Covens,' was just too good a book to put down. She had found the book in one of the many roadside gift shops where they had shopped on their way here. This was supposed to be THE best Unicorn Ranch and Resort in British Columbia.

"Camilla, where's your sister?" Camilla looked up from her book into the eyes of her mother.

Marcella looked at her somewhat surly teenager and smiled. All teens are the same. "Did you hear me? Your sister?"

Camilla tried to hide her book behind her. "She's over there." Camilla nodded in the direction of the fields.

"Ah, I see her." Marcella reached behind her daughter and pulled out the book.

"Wherever did you get this?"

Marcella flipped through the book and laughed. "This is very amusing. The publisher isn't a magical press. It looks like one put out by the mundane press."

"Can I have it back please?" Camilla frowned at her mother.

"Sure." Marcella tossed it to her. "The stories that humans make up about us. Don't believe that stuff. Coven rules and traditions aren't like that at all. As you should well know by now."

"I, uh, found it at one of the roadside shops we stopped at."

"I hope you didn't spend too much on it, then. It's time for lunch.

26

Come on back inside, I have people I want you to meet. Teegan! Lunch!" Marcella called for Teegan.

Teegan ran across the field and up the stairs. "Mom, did you see the Unicorns? They're marvelous!"

"I did, dear. They raise the best Unicorns this side of the Isle of Tir na nog. Later we will go see the young ones at the stables."

"Can we?" Teegan practically jumped into the air with joy.

"We can. Unicorns are very special beasts. They are one of the very few to adapt to the New World so hardily. Camilla, would you like to see the Unicorns, too?" Marcella peered at her oldest child.

"Can I just stay here and read? Unicorns are dumb." Camilla looked up from her book to look at her mother.

"Of course, dear. We are on vacation. Now come inside and have lunch. You can read later." Marcella pushed her two daughters toward the door. Alicorn Ranch was the largest of its kind in North America and a Blackmore family favorite for many years. The central lodge was three stories tall and could hold over twenty guests. The Magnus family owned both the ranch and the Spagyric Corporation that paid for it all.

Lunch, at least from Camilla's standpoint, was a trial of nerves. Everything was Unicorn or Unicorn themed.

"Do we have to eat...this?" Camilla pulled the top off her hamburger in disgust.

"It's beef, not Unicorn. It's just a name dear. You've had burgers before." Marcella looked over at her.

Camilla made a face. "It smells funny. Can I just eat dessert?"

Marcella shook her head. "No. Either eat your lunch or don't. No rewards for not eating in this house."

"Then I'm done." She pushed her meal away and left the table.

"Teegan, what's gotten into your sister? She didn't used to be so... surly."

Teegan shrugged her shoulders. "I don't know. She's been hanging out with the human kids at school and reading all the time. Can I have her burger if she doesn't want it?"

"Of course you may. What has she been reading?" Marcella scrutinized her daughter.

"Stuff. Heraldry, coven history, magick books, just books and things. She's been sort of secretive." Teegan dug into her sister's hamburger.

"Hmmm, keep an eye on her for me. OK?"

"I can try. She hates it when I spy on her." Teegan reached for more ketchup for her Unicorn fries.

"Do what you can. Thank you, Teegan." Marcella stared toward the now empty doorway with regret.

CAMILLA LEFT the dining hall and went back to the porch to read. Regardless of what her mother had said, this was the book she had been searching for!

"...among Witch families in the British Isles. Tradition holds that the oldest child inherits all things in the Coven. Only the European Covens differ. There, magical inheritance is based upon power and ability. The most powerful magick user is the one that inherits, regardless of birth order. In America, only a very few of the New England groups hold with European rules. Most have adopted the British tradition of inheritance. This author attempted to obtain documentation on the American Covens, particularly the Blackmore, Madl, and Carson ones. After negotiations failed, all attempts were dropped after the memory of the visits were purged from the editors of this book. Later attempts, using legal means..."

Ever since school last year she had been obsessed with finding the secret of inheritance. Her school was co-ed, with both magical and humans at the school together. The Blackmore family was something of an obsession with some of them, and they befriended her to learn more about Witches. They were surprised that as the eldest, she wasn't the heir apparent. So was Camilla. Asking her mother, Marcella, was useless. None of the so-called 'Elders' would give her a clear answer, either. The libraries at school and home hid the answer too. Only this book, so far, held the key. She needed to be the most powerful to get it all.

Camilla snapped her fingers, lighting a nearby candle. Her magic was just coming into its own. She made a mental note to study and learn. If she was good enough, her mother and the elders would choose her. No way could Teegan be as powerful. After all, SHE was the oldest child.

The sound of running feet broke her out of her thoughts. Teegan burst through the door and ran across the field toward the Unicorns.

Camilla studied her. Something would have to be done about Teegan. Something, soon.

GOOD THINGS, SMALL PACKAGES

T S PAUL

*This takes place during Agatha's and Cat's first year
at the Academy and when they first met Chuck.*

SCHOOL IS HARD.

I want to be here, don't get me wrong. I was homeschooled for most of my life. Primary school was a distant memory. My powers appeared at age four, but I didn't do anything with them until I was seven. That was when it all came crashing down. No more friends or birthday parties. I only interacted with my grandmother, family, and Fergus. A trash talking, nasty-minded, mini-Unicorn is not the best friend for a young girl Witch. To him, it's all about the horn. Trust me when I say that dress-up and tea parties with him were not the fun you would think. Grandmother's huge cat Zeus was more fun.

Here, I have found at least one good friend and a few who respect me. Having Cat as my roommate made up for some of what I missed out on as a child. This school was here to provide the background needed for government law enforcement service. It's supposed to be hard. This is my first year, and they are cramming a life's worth of math, science, and history into my brain. One of the things that has stuck in my mind is how special this place is. For many mundanes, if you want a job in law enforcement you go to school for it. There are law enforcement programs in most colleges. The problem is, those places don't normally accept Paranormals into their student bodies. Paranormal racism isn't against the law, at least not yet. We do have special needs and conditions. The FBI saw that, and addressed the need for paras in law enforcement. Weres make really good trackers and take-down specialists. The problem was, most lived on reservations, and educational requirements were non-existent. Something needed to change.

The FBI Academy became more of a boarding school for those students who qualified. It began as an experiment in diversity that evolved into a special place. Humans and paras could all go to school here together, learning to protect our country and its people. Several of the other government agencies have since done something similar. The CIA even has teenagers as Agents! This brings us back to my point. School lessons here are very intense and difficult. I have a lot of catching up to do. Especially since I am the only Magical person on campus.

The dorm that Cat and I live in is filled with Weres. There is also a very loose pack structure.

The few Alphas on campus kept control and formed mini-packs that might not stay together after graduation. Cat was one of the unaligned Weres. This meant she had yet to choose an Alpha or pack. Even though she was to be an agent, she still claimed her pack back home. Dominance tussles were a form of entertainment among the Weres.

Or at least that is what she keeps telling me.

Fights and power struggles were very common. Cat stayed far away from all that. She deliberately kept a low Were profile.

Personally, I don't blame her. She's short, blond, and has one heck of a temper. I have seen her throw things across the room that stuck. I would hate for her to be harmed in the games the boys insisted on playing.

"Cat, who is that guy?" We were watching one of the dominance fights from our dorm window.

"Who?" Cat stepped over to the window and peered through the blinds.

"The tall guy with the muscles. The one leaning up against that old green car."

"Oh, him. That's Charles. He's new like us this year. He's a WereCat, like me."

"Another cat? Where is the other cat?" Fergus, my familiar, came running out of his home on my desk. His shoe box sat in a prominent spot at the back.

"Fergus, calm down. The only cat in here is the one that lives here. Go watch TV or something."

The mini-Unicorn gave us a dirty look and snorted. He held his head high as he returned to his sport-shoe box. It was getting a bit worn around the edges. I made a mental note to go shopping and look for some new shoes for me. He could have the new box. Poor Fergus. Cats were his enemies, and we lived with one.

"That little guy cracks me up! You never told me why he hates cats?" I glanced at my roommate and smiled. It was pretty funny.

"Grandmother has a cat. His name is Zeus, and he's a Savannah Cat."

"I've heard of those. Aren't they really big house cats?"

"Right. Zeus is huge, and he thinks that Fergus is his personal plaything. I told you how Fergus came to live with me. What I didn't mention was part of the spell that shrank him also made him indestructible. He can really take a beating. To Zeus, he is an eternal plaything, much better than the field mice. Those fight back."

"They fight back?" She was looking at me like I was crazy.

"When animals live among magical people they pick up certain traits. A tribe of mice lives in Grandmother's garden. They have a tiny town and are armed with swords and armor. Fergus plays with them sometimes. He's scared of them. Zeus hunts them on occasion, but they can hurt him. Fergus doesn't fight back, so the cat uses him like a cat toy."

"They have a town?"

"I'm not supposed to know about it, but I found it when I was eight. Grandmother knew about them but told me to leave them alone. It's hidden, but I followed Zeus one day and found it. So Fergus hates all cats because of Zeus. Grams says that Zeus misses him."

Cat glanced back at the window and froze. "The fight is starting."

I looked out the window and watched as two large Weres began fighting. I recognized the larger of the two. He was one of the RAs down on the first floor of our dorm. He was wrestling with a tall, lanky Were that looked new. A rough circle was painted on the ground. The two men both removed their shirts and began trying to throw each other onto the ground. The tall Were's arms were not long enough to reach around the bulky residence assistant. He broke free easily and started punching the tall man.

I winced as the tall Were took a hard hit and landed flat on his back on the ground. The RA stood over him and smiled.

"So much for him. He gave up."

"How so?"

"You could tell his heart wasn't in it. He just wanted to attempt a fight rather than expose his throat and be done with it."

"So, he wanted to bow, but didn't want to seem weak?"

She looked at me and smiled. "Yes. You have been paying attention. Weakness is bad for Weres. Those who are the most dominant feel the urge to protect them."

"Like you."

She nodded. "Yes, like me. Wait...What? Damn it, Agatha!"

"Cat it's really obvious. I only see it because we are together so much. Is that why you avoid them?" I pointed out the window.

"I can't Agatha. I just can't fight. My cat wants me to, but I tell her no. It will work out." I watched as she gathered up her books to go study. I grabbed my bag and tagged along. The library was beckoning.

We were halfway there when we ran into Charles from the fight.

"Don't you two look cute. Want to go out for coffee? I have a car we could take." He practically appeared right in the middle of the sidewalk.

"We have to study. Please move out of the way." I asked politely.

"I wasn't talking to you, Witchy Poo. I was asking your short friend. She's tiny enough to be a dwarf. Is she a dwarf?"

"No, she's not a dwarf. Move out of the way, please. I really don't want to hurt you." I could feel my hand growing warm. Tossing a fireball at another student would be very bad.

"Leave her alone!" I looked over at Cat and could see the anger in her eyes. Uh, oh.

"What's the matter shorty, is the Witch your pet?" He stepped forward and physically pushed Cat. "Such a tiny little WereCat. You know you want to bend a knee to me. Let me see it. Show me your neck!"

"Go away! Leave Cat alone!" I really didn't want to attack him, but Cat was my friend.

"Agatha, stop!" Cat's eyes were slowly changing shape and color. "Leave us alone or meet me in the circle!"

The large Were started laughing. "The circle? You want to fight me, shorty?" He pushed Cat again.

Her voice much deeper now, she replied. "Yes. The circle. Three hours."

The Were looked surprised but nodded. "OK, challenge accepted. See you in three hours." He gave her another shove and headed back toward our dorm.

"Cat, what just happened?"

Cat's eyes were going back to normal. "I just accepted my first challenge."

"Can you win it?"

Cat was staring off into space. She slowly turned and smiled at me. "That guy has no idea who he's messing with. Wanna bet that those idiots on the lawn put him up to it?"

"I won't bet you, because I agree with you. They are scared of me."

"Come on. Let's go study. I have a fight this afternoon." We headed on toward the library. I was worried for her, but she didn't seem to be bothered with it.

Studying was harder than I thought it would be. All I could think about was the size of that big guy. I think she said his name was Charles. I had asked Cat about the size, and not in a dirty way! She explained that the laws of dimensional science didn't matter when it came to Weres. You turned into whatever you turned into. Some of the non-predator Weres could change into things like rabbits or weasels. A big person, little animal. It has driven more than one mundane scientist insane.

When it was time to leave, I told Cat I would protect her if she didn't want to fight. "Don't be silly, Aggy. This is what we do as Weres. It's about time I have at least one of these."

When we got back to the dorm, the Weres were already gathering. Cat was one of the few on campus that had not participated in any of the fights. Many of them had expected her to bow, not fight. We hurried back to the room and Cat stripped off her clothes. She dug around in her dresser and pulled out her gym clothes.

"Don't want to mess yours up?"

"Something like that. I intend to change into my cat form. I'm not large enough to take him as a human."

"Is your other form big enough? I know you explained this, but you are sort of smaller than him."

She smiled. "Don't worry. I've got this. No one has seen me change. No one living, that is. I can take him."

"OK, if you say so. If you want me to blast him, I will. I would zap him and make a new squirrel, but the Council is kind of down on me for doing that on purpose."

"That's OK. Come on, I can't be late." She grabbed a towel and threw it over her shoulder. I triggered the wards and closed the door behind us. I didn't bother to lock it. Only an idiot would try and rob us.

The challenge area was full of Weres of all sorts. A large fresh circle had been spray painted on the ground, and Charles was in the middle of it, showing off. He was flexing his muscles and preening for the few female Weres besides Cat.

I was an unknown factor here this year, and many of the older Weres gave me lots of room. A hole opened through the group fairly quickly when we arrived.

I nodded to one of the other girls at the edge of the ring. Her name was Lucy. She was a forensic tech major. Lucy set the spray can down and stepped over to me. "Sorry, Agatha. They have been pushing Chuck to challenge her. She's the only independent here."

Chuck. I loved it. That was going to be Charles' new name, whether he liked it or not. I'm not sure why Lucy bothered to whisper to me. Every Were on the field could hear what she said. Damn freaky hearing.

Our dorm's RA, the Alpha from the previous fight, stepped into the ring. He looked hard at Cat. She just smiled back at him. "I want a clean fight. No weapons other than those you were born with. Anything else is fair game. If you step out of the circle, you have ten seconds to get back inside or the match is forfeited. Do both of you understand?" He got nods from both Cat and Chuck. He stepped out of the ring, and the fight began.

Chuck charged Cat and grabbed her by her arm with an intent to toss her. She twisted out of his grasp and bent his thumb backward, making him scream out a curse. He snatched his hand away from her and backed up to the edge. I could see his finger move back into position as he healed. Cat turned and growled. Her eyes were changing shape.

Some of the Weres in the crowd looked concerned. Very few fights were fought in the other form. I could see Cat's arms begin to lengthen and fur peek out of her clothes. Chuck had one chance to pin her before she changed, and he took it. Cat growled louder as the big man tackled her, smashing her into the ground.

The Weres in the audience cheered. That was a classic move and usually resulted in a win for the one on top. Money began to change hands in the crowd as many assumed the fight was now over. Chuck seemed to grow in size until I realized it was Cat who was. With a screech, Chuck's entire body was thrown down, and a huge Cat rose from the ground. Big didn't begin to describe Cat's other form. She was massive! Saliva dripped from her mouth as she stalked her challenger. Chuck was still on the ground but faced away from her. Everyone in the crowd took a full step backward when she approached him.

Chuck woke up from the shock and blinked his eyes. The crowd nearest him were all but cowering in fear. He could smell the waves of fear coming off them. All of them were staring at him. He felt warm air and realized they weren't staring at him but over him. He turned his head and began to scream!

Cat's large, saber tooth head was inches from his body. She was breathing her hot breath on him as she held him down with a dinner plate sized paw. His entire upper torso would fit in her mouth, so she spread her jaws and held them over his groin area. The big man and about half the crowd instinctively pinched their legs together. Chuck tilted his head back and showed his throat. The big cat huffed at him and ran toward the dorm. The fight attendees stumbled to get out of her way. I stepped into the ring and picked up her clothing. No one spoke to me.

It was one thing to worry about me. Now they had her to worry about, too. She might be small, but she could be a real monster if she needed to be.

DON'T FEED THE UNICORN!

T S PAUL

This story takes place during Agatha's and Cat's first year at the FBI Academy. Between Book 0 and Book 1.

"EVER WONDER what a mini-Unicorn does all day? Want to find out?" I chuckled as I wrapped Chuck's foot.

"Do I have to?"

"No. But you cannot walk on that foot for at least twenty-four hours. Don't give me that, 'if I shift it will heal faster BS.' I know better. It still has to have time to heal, shifted or not. Now, it's the weekend so no classes. Cat and I are going into town to hit some malls and maybe see a movie. No, you can't go. It's a chick day, not a bro day. Suck it up."

"But, why do I have to stay here? I could go back to my room. My roommate can watch me." Chuck looked up at me with those baby blue eyes.

"Nope, not going to fall for it. Fergus does that every time he wants something. Your roommate is how you ended up like this. What in the name of the Gods did you think you were doing, jumping off that gazebo onto a moving car?"

"It was a dare? Besides, I did the math on it. It should have worked. The only thing I can think of is the drag coefficient related to the driver's acceleration. Hmmm." He cocked his head and closed his eyes.

"Sounds like too stupid to know better. No, your roommate is not suitable. If you like, I can get Cat to give you a direct order to stay here?"

"Oh, No. Staying here is fine. There's a game on today anyway. I'm good."

"Uh, huh. So, a few Fergus ground rules. Don't feed the Unicorn. He's pretty self-sufficient, but he likes to binge eat, and it's not good for him. So no matter how much he begs, don't feed him. You have our numbers, but don't call unless the building is on fire. See ya." I picked up my bag and left the room. Cat had the keys to Chuck's Riviera, and we were going shopping!

"I THOUGHT she'd never leave. That looks painful, what happened to you?" Chuck looked over at the little red barn, but Fergus was standing on the coffee table looking up at him.

"I jumped off a gazebo onto a moving car. It was a stunt from that new Impossible Stunts TV show. Jake, my roommate, figured as a Were I was a bit faster than the human stunt man. I think my math was off somehow. I slipped and landed wrong."

"That's where you messed up. You have to keep all four feet firmly on the ground like the Gods intended. None of that jumping stuff."

"I've seen you jump before."

"Of course you have. I have equine blood in me. We like to jump.

40

One of my cousins, twice removed, used to participate in competition. He was a dresser champion."

Chuck looked down at the tiny Unicorn. "I think you mean dressage."

"That is what I said, Dresser. He jumped over fences and stuff."

"It's called dressage."

"What is?"

"The jumping. It's called dressage."

"I know that. Why are you telling me about it?"

Chuck just covered his face with his hands and groaned.

An hour later Chuck had the TV on, a root beer in his hand, and all was nice and comfortable on Cat's bed. The game was about to begin when Fergus hopped up on the bed.

"Hey, can I have a root beer?"

"No. How did you get up here?" Chuck looked over the edge of the bed. "It has to be a foot and a half."

"I jumped."

"No, really? How did you do it?"

"I jumped. It's the same way I open the door."

Chuck pointed at the door. "That door?"

"Do you see another door? Of course, that door."

"Why do you need the door open?"

"So I can get lunch. Do you want something? It's on me."

"I'd love a pizza or a couple of pizzas, but I'm broke right now. I have snacks." He held up a bag of popcorn.

The toy barn made a mooing sound as the door opened and then closed. Chuck stared at the desk for a moment. "Hey, Fergus? How did you get up there? It's got to be four or five feet!"

"I told you. I jumped!"

Chuck stared at the desk and tried to do the math in his head. The number of pounds per square inch that the Unicorn would have to compress to jump that high or the possibility that Unicorns could fly? He was torn. Chuck was starting to formulate a third option when there was a knock at the door. Hopping over to it he looked thru the peephole. There was a pizza guy out there. He opened the door and stared at the red and black striped man.

"Fergus in?"

"How do you know Fergus?" The pizza man handed Chuck two pizza boxes and a Styrofoam container.

"I make deliveries here all the time. Fergus is cool."

The pizza man turned and walked away. "Hey, what do we owe you?"

"It's already paid for!"

Chuck closed the door and stared at the pizza in his hands. "Fergus, how did you do that?"

"I called them from my phone. I use it as a TV, but it's still a phone."

"How did you pay?"

"I charged it to the phone account. I do it almost every day."

"But how? Agatha must see the bill."

"Nope. Cat helped her get the phones, but Grandma pays the bill on it. You're not going to rat me out, are you?"

Looking at the free pizza in his hand Chuck said, "Nope."

WHEN CAT and I returned from our girl's day, we found Chuck sound asleep on the bed in front of the TV. Fergus was asleep next to him.

"I wonder what they did all day?"

I smiled at Cat. "I have no idea. Who knows what Fergus does all day?"

TRICK OR TREAT

T S PAUL

Cat's and Agatha's first Halloween at the Academy.

FALL IS my favorite time of the year. It's not just because of Halloween. In my world, we call it Samhain and pronounce it like 'Sowen.' It's the dark time, the end of the solar year. In the ancient world, it marked the end of harvest and the beginning of Winter. It is during this long night that the veil between the worlds is the thinnest. Many of my folk believe it is the time for communicating with the dead. We leave offerings of food and other items to honor those lost to us by death in the last year. Mundanes borrowed the idea of knocking on doors to beg for treats. They used to play tricks to entertain and gather food for the harvest feasts from the people in ancient times. It is what Trick-or-Treating has become today. As a child, I loved to dress up and hand out candy with Grandmother. We are Witches. It is our duty and tradition to honor both the Gods and those who have gone before us.

That was all back in Maine. Here in Virginia, at the Academy, things are a little bit different. This is my second year at the FBI school. Cat and I volunteered for the Harvest Faire on the Marine

Base. Director Mills thought it might provide some goodwill with them. So we set up booths and helped to provide a safe holiday for the children and dependents of the Military. Both Cat and I thought it was a wonderful idea. Which is why we made Chuck do all the toting and hauling.

"I don't see why I have to do all this. Isn't it your jobs, as organizers of this thing?" Chuck could barely be seen under the tables and chairs we loaded on top of him.

"It is, but we are just little girls, and you are all big and strong, Chuck." I made a girlish giggle as I said that.

"Uh, huh. Sure, you are. I've seen you do some crazy stuff there, Witchy Poo."

I made a face and stuck my tongue out at him. He knows I hate being called that.

"Just set that stuff here on the curb." Chuck set everything down. I gave him another little girl look. "Just one more little trip? Cat needs help getting the cooler and food over here. I promise I will call in that order so you and the guys can have your pizza party."

He took in my pitiful look and deflated. "Fine. Just one more trip. I want pepperoni," he grumped.

It ended up being three more trips, but Chuck was a good sport about it. I called in the order and Anchors a Weigh said they'd sent their guy over with pizza for the boys. Cat and I laughed that we got set up early, before anyone else. We figured if we were going to be in charge, we should set a good example of the right way to set up a booth.

The forensic group was the next to set up. They had a neat booth with fingerprint painting and gummy worm cupcakes. I thought I even saw gelatin molds in the shape of brains over there. The kids would love that! Our Academy Chef and his crew set up a warming station this year. They left the goodies to us. His crew was planning to hand out coffee and spice teas to warm up the parents and kids. Fall in Virginia can be cold at night. All my friends volunteered when they heard we were going to run things this year. The last booth to arrive was the recruiting one. The B's were running it this year. They were so cute dressed in minion outfits. They kept running over to us saying 'Hello' all the time. I can't be the only one that thinks they look like snack cakes with feet, can I?

"Hey, it's starting to get dark." I looked up at the sky.

"Yup, it is. Just like last night."

Cat gave me a push that almost made me lose my footing. I forget how strong she is. "No, you said you would light the booth up when it got dark."

"Oh, that. It's not dark yet." I smiled to myself. She was fun to mess with.

She coughed and pointed at the booth. It was hard to take an elf with cute, sparkly wings seriously, but I didn't want to see the giant cat version of her here.

"Fine. It's not quite dark enough, but I can do a few things. Do you want fog too?" We had these really cool pumpkins the Wolf boys back at the dorm helped us carve. We set the pumpkins in front of the booth and on each corner. I thought it might be cool to have scary lights in them and fog drifting around. I knew the spell for those effects, but had not done them without Grandmother's supervision yet.

I said a small prayer to my Goddess of choice and recited the spell from memory to get the spooky flickering lights. When I opened my eyes, the pumpkins all had really cool purple flames that acted just like a real candle.

"Damn, Aggy that is so cool!" Cat stuck her hand in one of the pumpkins and wasn't burned.

"It's an illusion. I set a time limit for three hours, but they might burn longer than that. That was the easy part. I've never attempted the fog spell. Are you sure you want it?"

"Go for it. What's the worst thing that can happen?" I was glad Cat had so much faith in me.

I could think of a lot of things, but I went for it anyway. If I was going to overcome my spell issues I needed to do actual spells. I closed my eyes and concentrated on the idea of pumpkins that had wisps of fog coming from them. Very slowly, I cast the spell I created. I felt the Magick leave my body and go...somewhere. I opened one eye and stared at the front of the booth. Tiny wisps of fog were starting to come out of all the pumpkins.

"I did it!" I started jumping around. Cat jumped with me until we attracted too much attention. My creepy artificial fog was slowly gliding along the ground, giving the entire area a spooky appeal.

We heard voices and looked to see children and parents streaming into the square. Our booth attracted the most children. It was a good thing we stocked up on cookies! For almost a full hour we talked to parents and kids as they came past our booth. Finally, Director Mills made an appearance.

"Girls! Your booth is awesome! I love the lights. The fog is such a cool effect. Have you had a good response?"

We looked at each other and laughed. "Yes! We packed twenty cases of wrapped cookies, and we have barely two left. I think every kid in town has one."

"Wonderful! How are the other booths doing?"

"The last time I looked, the Chef and his crew were having a party over there. The Techs got rave reviews for their brains and creepy fingers. Everyone is having a great time." I smiled at her. This carnival reminded me of home.

"I'm going to circulate." She thanked us again, and we turned back to the horde of children.

Many of the costumes stuck out. There were Witches and Weres everywhere. Cartoon characters were popular this year too, as were some TV show classics. I found myself giving the trek finger salute, and saying I was a leaf on the wind to several children and adults. We were down to our last couple of cookies when two really cute little girls approached us.

"Trick or treat!"

"Hi there, would you girls like a cookie?"

"Yes, please." I smiled at the short blond girl. She was dressed in a military outfit that I didn't recognize. In her right hand, she held a flaming volleyball along with her treat bag.

"What is your costume? I like your ball."

"I'm Athena Lee! She's my favorite space character. This is Wilson!" She held up the ball.

"I don't know that one. Is she a TV show?"

The little girls looked at me seriously. "No silly, she's the hero of my favorite book series."

I looked up at the girl's mother, and she smiled at me. Wow, kids still read books? I looked over at her friend. She was dark-haired and was dressed in a black Cat-suit. I could see vampire teeth in her mouth and figured she was from one of my favorite movie series.

"Who are you tonight?" I expected her to say Selene but got a surprise.

"I'm Bethany Anne. She is the Queen!" The little girl gave me an imperious look. Oh boy, did her parents have a tough one there!

Her mother smiled at me too. "She's the heroine in a book series she reads. Her father left them out where she could find them, and she read the whole series. Between you and me, I popped him a good one for that. They have way too much bad language in them."

"At least she's reading. Sounds like you have a smart one there."

"We do, thanks." The parents and their book reading brood stepped away. I looked at Cat. She was half asleep. It had been a long couple of hours.

"Agatha? How did you get the statue to make fog?" I spun around at Chuck's voice.

"Hey, Chuck. Come to help us break down?"

"No. Crap. I guess I can help." He looked at the ground. Poor Chuck.

"Here, I saved you a cookie." I handed him the last one.

"So how did you do it?"

"Do what?" I asked.

"Get the statue to make smoke."

"What statue?"

"The one over there." He pointed past the booth down the path to the park.

"There's a statue over there?" This was my first time in this part of the reserve.

"Yeah, it's called Pumpkin Square for a reason. There is a fall-themed statue in the park with a big pumpkin on it."

"Uh, oh." I tried to remember the lines of the spell I cast. I had been facing in that direction when I cast. How was I supposed to know there was a stone pumpkin over there?

"Agatha, what's wrong?" Cat saw the look of shock on my face.

"Did you know this park is called Pumpkin Square, and that there is a stone pumpkin over there?" I pointed to the park.

"Yes. Why?"

"You know that pumpkin spell I did?"

"You didn't!" she squeaked.

All I did was stare at her.

"Can you turn it off?"

"I don't know how! The way the spell works is it causes the pumpkins to rot quickly, and the spell disappears as they do. A stone pumpkin would last forever."

"What do we do? Should we tell someone?" Cat looked around the square. Everyone was ignoring us as they broke everything down.

"Run?"

Cat laughed until she realized I was serious. "Maybe they won't notice?"

"It might wear off. Let's pack up and get out of here." We packed as quickly as possible, throwing the smoking pumpkins in the dumpster.

Chuck grabbed all he could and headed for our borrowed van. We passed the Director on the way out.

"Thanks for all your work, girls!"

"We had fun, Director Mills. See you back at the Academy." We loaded the borrowed van and drove back.

"Do you think your spell will wear off?"

"No. We are in big trouble."

"What's this 'we,' Witch girl?" Cat smiled at me. I knew she was kidding.

I was almost asleep when the call came in. Turning my phone back on, I grimaced. Over a dozen messages from the Director just about set my phone on fire. It seems the local fire department was called out to extinguish a dumpster fire and a statue that would not stop 'smoking' no matter how much water they poured on it.

Oops?

PRANCER

T S PAUL

Sometimes Unicorns should be seen and not heard.
Or both!

I WAS sound asleep when I first heard it. Tap, tap, tap, tap, tappitty tap. I blinked my eyes a few times and looked over at my digital clock. Three AM? What by all the Gods is that noise?

"Cat, is that you making that noise to drive me more insane?" I didn't even look in her direction. I just stared at the ceiling.

"It's not me. I thought it was you, Agatha! I was getting ready to throw something at you."

The noise started up again. Tap, tap, tap, tap, tappitty tap. Both Cat and I turned our heads and tracked in on the sound. It was coming from Fergus's barn.

"If he's doing this to piss me off again, I swear it will be tiny Unicorn steaks for lunch!" Cat had sat up and was glaring over at me.

I clicked on the bedside light and instantly regretted it. "Ugh, light." I rubbed my eyes and stared at Cat for a moment. The noise started up again. Tap, tap, tap, tap, tappitty tap.

"Fergus! What in the nine hells are you doing in there!" I stood and walked the three steps or so over to his barn. Not bothering with the door, I opened up the top and peered inside.

"Hey, I'm naked in here!"

"You're always naked. Stop using that as an excuse. What in the name of Elton John are you doing in there?"

I looked down into the barn, and he had cleared a space in the middle for a dance floor. There was actually a disco ball hanging from the loft. That wasn't the strangest thing in the barn, however.

"What have you done to yourself?"

"What do you mean?"

"You know exactly what I mean!" Cat tapped me on the shoulder.

"What has he done now?" She had gotten out of bed and was staring at the barn.

"Take a look for yourself."

Cat pushed past me and peered down into the barn. "HAHA-HAHA! He's your Unicorn, but that's one of the funniest damn things I've ever seen." She was still laughing as she put on a robe and left the room.

My normally white with blue hair Unicorn was now pink with violet hair and sparkles! "What happened to your Mohawk? Are those hair extensions? Where do you get hair extensions for a Unicorn?"

"I have resources."

"Why oh why, are they pink and sparkly?"

"It's for my dance routine?"

"Why are you dancing?"

"I got the idea from my new favorite TV show?"

"What TV show? Are you wearing makeup? How did you put lipstick on? You don't have hands!" He looked like some sort of cartoon show horse.

"It's called 'Prancing Pony Makeovers.' I found it on late-night TV. They get older ponies and give them a complete makeover."

"Really? And why are you dancing?"

"I saw it on another show. 'Dancing with the Rodeo Stars.' It looked like fun!"

"That's it, no more late-night TV for you! I'm calling Grandmother and canceling your phone."

"I won't dance anymore at night, I promise! Don't take my only source of entertainment, please?"

Looking down at his pitiful made-up face, I grimaced and caved. "Fine. No more dancing and I mean it. I'll let Cat eat you, if you do."

Cat came back into the room and got back into bed. "Is he going to stop?"

"Yup. He promised this time. You can eat him if he starts doing it again." I laid back down and turned off the light. As my eyes closed, I thought to myself, where DID he get the makeup from?

JACKS ON THE RUN!

T S PAUL

This is Chuck's story of how he transported the Jackalopes to Kentucky and what happened afterward.

How HARD CAN IT BE? Hire two FBI Academy students to move thirty pairs of Jackalopes in a rental truck back to Kentucky. Jackalopes, it seems, are smarter than the average Bunny.

"Chuck how many of these things did we catch?"

"I'm not sure. Maybe a hundred?" Chuck was scratching his head. He was standing outside the FBI dorm in a field filled with pissed off Jackalopes in cheap rabbit cages.

"Do we have to give them all away? I mean, I could go for a Jack and cheese right about now." Mongo was eying both the grill and the Jacks.

"Down Mongo! We'll stop at KFC on the way out of town. Remember how hard it was to catch these things? I'm not doing that again on purpose."

"Aww, you could just get that cute Witch friend of yours to magic you up some more." Mongo poked him with a grin.

"She's not MY Witch, dude. She would not find that funny at all. We are Packmates, that's all."

"You might have a better chance with her than with Cat," his friend hinted.

The big shifter started laughing. "Cat? She would make me eat my own hand if I even asked her out. Have you seen her other form?"

"I heard the story, but she can't be THAT big, can she?" The WereBear just shook his head as he peered at one of the Jacks in the cage.

"She's scary, is what she is. I must have been the world's biggest idiot to have even thought of challenging her. She's an Alpha, so I assumed she might be big. I had no idea! I'm lucky my cat yielded."

The Jack in the cage charged and got his antlers stuck. Startled, Mongo jumped back with a yell.

"Watch those things! They bite." Chuck grinned at the antics of his friend. WereBears were a bit rare and were almost never seen outside of The Dominion of Canada or Alaska. Too many Mundanes got them confused with real bears and shot them. Mongo's family was a bit special. They escaped Russia by the hair on their head during the end of the Demon War. Theirs was one of the last refugee boats before the Soviets cracked down on the country.

The WereBears were too large to be useful to the Empire of Japan. Clothing was impossible to find, and they couldn't speak the language very well. Mongo's father found work on a ship headed to the east, and he booked passage for the rest of the family. They almost went to the Dominion of Canada, but the laws for Were in the British Empire were too strict, so America it was.

"I like rabbits that fight back! You're sure we can't eat some of these?" Mongo begged.

Chuck sighed. "We really only need thirty pairs to take to Kentucky."

"I'll get the grill fired up!" Mongo ran off toward the dorm. Chuck just laughed to himself. Agatha helped to create a monster this time. Checking his phone, he smiled. Jacob should be here pretty soon with the panel truck Cat's father, Mr. Moore, rented. They would pick the thirty best pairs and load up. It should only take a couple of hours. Mongo might be right, a Jack and cheese sandwich might be good about now.

A bit more than several hours later...

"Why did you let me eat that last one?" Mongo rubbed his bloated stomach for the fifth time.

"Let you? Mongo, you told everyone you were going for the record. Are you going to be OK? I can stop for some Pepto or something." The big bear was slumped over in his seat, still rubbing his stomach.

"Nyet! Just drive. I'm fine."

"Sounds good, let's get the party on the road. It's about eleven hours to Cadiz." Chuck put the truck in gear and stepped on the gas. Robert, Cat's dad, had paid him to transport the Jacks to his home in Cadiz, Kentucky. Why he wanted them was still a puzzle to Chuck.

Two hours later...

"Ugh! Dude, did you have to fart inside the truck!" Chuck was standing on the side of the road gasping for breath. Mongo let one fly a couple of minutes ago that made him almost drive off the road.

"No more Jack and cheese for you! I'm surprised you're still walking around, stinking like that!" Chuck grabbed hold of a road sign and tried not to puke his guts out. The road sign said 'Shenandoah National Park, next ten miles.'

"It's not that bad." Mongo was flapping his shirt trying to fan out the truck cab.

"You must be immune, then. Since we're stopped, let's check on the Jacks." They stepped around the back and pulled up the door.

Several large, horned, and furry creatures knocked both young men to the ground.

"What the hell! Catch them!" Chuck yelled at Mongo. The fleeing Jacks were out the door and past the two of them faster than any regular rabbits on Earth.

"They are gone, Chuck! How did they get out?"

"You're asking me? I thought you locked the cages?"

"I did." The back of the truck sagged as Mongo's large form climbed inside. Ten of the previously neatly stacked cages were down on the truck deck, smashed and broken open.

"What escaped, males or females?"

"I don't know. How am I supposed to tell that?" Mongo stared at Chuck in surprise.

"Remember when we sexed them before the cookout? I told you to put them in the truck that way, so we could tell Mr. Moore which was which."

"Oh, that. Yeah, about that. I sort of got the newbs to load the truck for me." Mongo looked down at the floor.

"Dude. That is so not cool. Now we have no idea which is which! Damn it, Mongo, why?"

"I wanted to go get a beer, so they said they would load the truck if I brought them some, too."

"You bought freshmen beer? Mongo they're just kids! You're in the FBI now, not high school!"

"I know, I know. I didn't actually give them any. They do look young this year, don't they?"

"Which newbs were they?" Chuck now shook his head at his friend.

"They're the ones in the Sea Scout program. They called themselves Tritons or something."

"I know the ones you're talking about. Tritons are what male mermaids are called."

"Really? I thought those were only sailors like that kids' movie." Mongo stacked the broken cages in the corner of the truck.

"That's only legend. Or at least I think it is. We could ask the Mer sisters. They would tell you if you asked. I think they like you."

"Thelma, Molly, and Geia, those sisters? No, thank you. They would eat me alive!" Mongo shuddered.

"We need to get moving. Let's go."

Mongo drummed his fingers on the dashboard as they got back on the highway. "Do you think we will get into trouble for letting those escape?"

"No, I don't think so. What worries me is where they got out. That was a Tennessee State Park! If Agatha gets in trouble, I'm telling her it was your fault. Maybe it was only males that escaped."

Eight hours later at a ranch house in Cadiz...

"You made it! Good work, Chuck!" Robert Moore was dressed in hunting gear.

"Yes, Sir. This is Mongo Medved. He goes to school with us."

Robert looked the tall student up and down and gave a sniff. "Bear?"

"Yes, Sir." Mongo looked down at the WereCat Alpha.

"I think my daughter may have mentioned you. It's surprising to see a bear this far south. Most of you like the colder parts of the country. Do you?"

"Yes, Sir. My parents tried living up north, but they said it was too much like Russia. Father likes to say that there are too many chefs in the kitchen up there."

Robert started laughing. "That, young man, is a good description of the Ursa Packs. A good one indeed. I like your father already. What does he do?" Robert Moore looked keenly at the young Were.

"He runs one of the best barbecue restaurants in Huntsville, Alabama. It's called Bare Naked Butts. Mom hates the name, but he's about four blocks from the college at home, so business is good."

Still laughing, Robert clapped the bear on the back. "I see a trip to Huntsville in my future. If the FBI gig doesn't work out for you, come see me, Mongo. I can always use smart, well-trained Weres."

Mongo pulled his head back in surprise. "Really? Thank you, Sir."

"It's Robert. Call me Robert. You too, Chuck. I know you technically belong to Catherine, but call me if you need something. Now let's see what you brought me."

"Uh, we had a small problem just before we left Virginia. Some of them escaped."

"Did they really? How many?" Robert looked at Chuck as he pulled the door open.

"Ten total. We aren't sure how many of each. They sort of got mixed up when the truck got loaded." The Jacks began to thrash in the cages as the door came up. Several had antlers already stuck.

"So how many do you have?" He stared into the truck.

"We have about fifty of them in here."

"Fifty? Excellent. That should be enough."

"Can I ask why you wanted them? If it's a barbecue, we could have cleaned and prepared them back at school."

"No, it's not for a cookout. I'm going to release them. The game is drying up in our area. The Mundanes still hunt here, and much of the area over there is state property." He pointed off to the west. "They should make for good hunting for our people don't you think? There isn't a sign, but this is a private lodge our Pack runs as an investment. Big money to be made in hunts."

"Won't the government say anything?" Chuck frowned at his Pack leader's father.

"Nope. If you read the laws that were passed on the subject, private land is exempt. It's all legal. Except for maybe the ones that got away. With any luck, they were all males and won't breed. Come on inside. My crew will unload the truck for you. Maybe you can give me some Jack recipes."

Seven hours away, several pregnant Jackalope females hopped through a protected forest. The only predators that could have prevented their spread had been hunted to extinction.

CAT'S NIGHT OUT

T S PAUL

While Agatha was on her Probi mission, Cat had one of her own. A serial killer stalked the south, killing entire families in their sleep. Sometimes it takes a Monster to catch a Monster.

Chapter One

WHEN I WAS TOLD I was going 'into the pool' I assumed it wasn't a literal pool. I was almost right. This was not what I expected my new internship with the investigative branch of the FBI to entail. I wanted to be doing something like my pack-mates Agatha and Chuck were doing. It didn't matter to the Agents in charge that I was a graduate, an Alpha, or even a girl. I was a Newb and a Probi. My current assignment was to review previous cases and 'get a clue' to methodology. I sat in a room among a pool of other Agents in the same situation. Many of these people were graduates of the other half of the Academy, the one for older applicants. I was the youngest person in the room.

"Hey, hand me a new box."

"Are you speaking to me?" I stared at the older Agent sitting across from me. He was staring at the pile of file boxes next to me.

"See anyone else next to you? Hand me another box."

"I guess they don't teach courtesy at the Academy." I grabbed a heavy looking box and tossed it at him.

"Oof! Hey, that was heavy!" He set it down at his feet and started picking through it. "You're new. Expect to be here for a while. They are very picky for something like this."

"Aren't we all Agents?"

"We are. But new Agents are basically gophers until someone signs off on your promotion to actual Agent. Expect to be getting coffee a lot." He didn't look to be a happy soul.

"How long have you been a Probi?"

"Two years. I was a sheriff's deputy in a little Georgia town called Hahira. I wanted to expand my knowledge base and joining the FBI was a way to do it. I've been stuck in this room since graduation!"

"Sorry I asked." I smiled at him.

"It has its advantages, though. I have a nice place with digital TV and a water bed. Would you like to come over and check it out?"

I couldn't believe this guy was trying to pick me up, and during a case, even. It irritated me enough to let the Alpha in me show just a bit.

"Grrrrrrr."

"Did you just growl at me? You must be a real tiger in bed! We get a lunch break in a few minutes. We can get over there and be back in plenty of time."

Claws shot out of my hands and ripped the box I was holding completely in half. My eyes gleamed yellow and my growl got louder. "Gooo Away!"

The older man finally took the hint and nearly fell out of his chair. He left a wet spot as he ran from the room.

***

"Agent Nixon? We need you to add a probationary Agent to your team."

"Sir, a probi? Now? Isn't this a serial killer we are chasing? Why add a newb now?"

The Special Agent in Charge just stared at his most senior Agent. "You know as well as I do that when Washington speaks, we listen."

"Do I need to just pick one or is there someone special?"

"Special. Washington has their eye on this one for some reason. Just do it. Have her file notes or something."

"Fine. What is her name?"

I WAS on my third box when the door opened. I glanced up and it wasn't one of the swimmers from the pool. Calling them swimmers made me feel a bit better. Ever since I chased off the masher, the others had been distancing themselves from me. I now sat completely alone at the rear of the room.

"Is there a Catherine Moore in here?" The Agent at the door looked completely bored.

Everyone in the room looked around at each other. Catherine Moore? Who was that?

"I'm Catherine Moore." I raised my arm and stood up. Every eye in the room focused upon me.

"Come along, then. You have been reassigned."

I picked my way through the 'swimmers' in the room. Being a Were, I could hear them grumbling and griping under their breath as I passed.

"You're a short one. Head toward the main room and hang a left. That is where we are meeting." He held the door for a moment and then walked in the opposite direction.

I followed the directions and knocked on the door as I entered the room. Four Agents sat around a table covered in piles of paperwork. Two whiteboards and a clear case board surrounded the table. They too were covered with pictures and documents. This group was the lead on the Marietta slasher.

"Hello?" The seated Agents all looked over at me. "I was told by the other Agent to come in here?"

"Oh good. You must be the Probi assigned to us. I'll have a ham and cheese on wheat. Don't forget the chips. I prefer baked, not fried. Diet soda any kind is fine." The other Agents all called over an order too. I stared at them for a moment and then left.

"We have a Probi? Why?"

"Orders from Washington. No choice, Nixon, already tried to get out of it."

"She's kind of small. We can always use a coffee runner." The table all laughed.

I heard every bit of the conversation as I left. None of the Agents gave me money, so I assumed that I was supposed to pay for this stuff. Not going to happen. I walked back to the pool and grabbed some of the take-out menus off the bulletin board outside.

The Agents were still sitting around the table when I walked back inside. Agent Nixon had joined them. They were all laughing about some joke. None of the documents had been opened or even moved.

I set the menus down on the table and grabbed one of the empty chairs.

"What are these for?" The female Agent who had ordered the ham sandwich stared at me.

"Order your own lunch. I'm an Agent, not a delivery person."

A couple of the other Agents giggled at my statement. Agent Nixon just glared at me. "You are what we say you are, probi!"

"If you want me off your case, tell your boss." I smiled at his discomfort. "I'm staying."

The chuckling Agents all stared and the laughter fell away. Nixon shook his head. "You know I can't do that?"

"I do. Now do you people actually work or just sit here?"

"Hey! I resent that accusation! This case has us stumped is all.

We know that the Unsub is a family annihilator, but we can't get a handle of why or how he's picking them."

"Can I see the evidence?" I looked Nixon in the eye.

"Sure." He pointed at the boards. "The Unsub killed the Smith family in their home in the wee hours of the morning. Using what we assume is a razor, he cut the screens on the second floor's hallway window and crawled in. We didn't find any trace of a ladder, so we assume he is athletic. Using either a razor or dagger, he killed the parents first. The husband bled out while the Unsub 'played' with the wife. Her throat was cut last. The children died in their sleep, never waking to the violence happening in the next room. We suspect he snuck in and broke their necks. The autopsies were inconclusive as to how it was done. Their older son found them the next morning. He had been away at college. His screaming alerted the neighbors."

Nixon pointed at the second board. "The next case was three blocks away, the following week. Similar entry technique was used. Razor to the window. This time he killed the children first. He may have been surprised or it was just opportunity. The parents weren't asleep. They were tax accountants and had a new client. They were surprised in their home office and fought back. We found defensive wounds on the husband and on the wife. The coroner says the same weapon was used for both families. It looks like it might be a serial killer."

"Have we notified the BAU?" I studied both boards.

"We have. They are tied up dealing with a mass murder in Alaska. A hunter or hunters went on a killing spree in a small town up there. This one is all ours."

I tapped my finger against my lips. "OK. What is the common link beyond method?"

The Agents all looked at me. "Nothing we can find. The two families have nothing in common, other than location."

"Nothing at all?" I studied the pictures and notes. Each pile on the table corresponded to a point on the boards.

"Nothing. We have gone over these files numerous times."

"Do you mind if I take a look?" I asked them.

"We don't have much choice. Go ahead." He and the others stepped out of the room and went, I assumed, to lunch. I dug into the records and files making my own piles as I went.

Several hours passed and I barely noticed when the others came back. The documentation was very organized and complete, almost too complete.

"See anything interesting?" Agent Nixon asked as he pulled a chair out across from me.

I looked up into the eyes of Agent Nixon. "Yes and no. The report mentions that outside the house a dog was killed in the back-yard of the first family. Presumably by the Unsub as he climbed up the back of the house."

"Yes. The dog was a big German Shepherd."

"The problem I have is there is no food or water bowls out for the dog, or even a place for it to sleep outside. When asked the neighbors said they didn't have a dog. So where did it come from?"

"The second family is very similar. A dead dog was found inside the house along with the family. Was an autopsy done on either of the animals found?"

Agent Nixon dug into the pile of reports in front of him. "The bodies were sent to a local Vet, but I don't see a report here." He looked over at the female Agent who had first spoken to me. "Ramirez? Did you follow up with that Vet about the dead dogs?"

She looked up and smiled at Agent Nixon. "I have his report here somewhere. Was there a question about them?"

"Yes. What killed the dogs?" Nixon asked her.

"They had obvious slash wounds. We assumed that was what killed them." Ramirez relied with another smile.

I rolled my eyes. "Did you check or even read the report?"

"It's right here somewhere." She dug into the file in front of her. After a moment she looked up at us and blushed. "I guess I didn't get it from the man. He explained it to me though. Let me give them a call."

Agent Nixon frowned at her. "Go down there yourself and get the report. Take Jones with you. Don't come back without the report."

Agent Jones looked up from the sandwich he was cramming into his mouth. "Hmmph?"

Nixon glared at Jones and yelled, "go with Ramirez. Get moving!"

He looked back at me. "Good work. Did you find anything else we missed?"

"Just some inconsistencies in the report about the weapon used. The slashes don't look as though they were done with a razor. Have you had a Were sniff the crime scene?" I asked him.

"There aren't all that many Weres in the Bureau around here. Most take Western assignments. I can request one," Nixon took the report from me and scanned it.

"I'm an Alpha WereCat, Agent Nixon. I can do it. Are the scenes still undisturbed?" I informed him.

Nixon's eyes wend wide for just a moment. Looking to his left he spoke. "They are supposed to be. Tony? We haven't released the scenes, have we?"

The other male Agent looked up from his phone. "Did you need something boss?"

"Are the two crime scenes still secure?" Nixon asked again.

Tony opened up the file in front of him and read for a moment. "They are. The surviving family have requested access but we've been denying it."

"Good. Pass a message to the locals. We are going to reinspect the crime scenes but with Agent Moore's help this time," Nixon replied.

Tony frowned. "Didn't we already inspect them?"

I was still reading the forensic reports when Agents Ramirez and Jones returned with the vet report. They handed it to Agent Nixon and there was a bit of muttered conversation. I'm not sure why they bothered since I could hear it all anyway.

"HERE IS THE REPORT, Albert. Why did I have to go all the way down there? He could have just as easily faxed it to us." Ramirez remarked.

Nixon took the file but didn't open it. "Did you read it?"

"No. It was just two dead animals. The Vet already explained the details. We need to concentrate on the family deaths, not a couple of animals." Ramirez explained.

"When you spoke to the Vet did he say anything about the autopsies he did? Anything that leapt out at him would be helpful. Jones?" Nixon looked at both his agents.

Jones looked down at his notes. "He said the first one died from wounds received."

"What about the other one, did he not do an autopsy on it?" Nixon asked.

"Umm, I told him not to. Just to do the exam. It was obvious they died as result of the unsub's attack." Ramirez patted her hair and examined her fingernail.

"Damn it! Jones, what happened to the animals afterwards? Can we still order a follow up autopsy?" Nixon yelled.

Jones looked surprised to be called upon again. "Uh, I think he said something about cremation. It's in the report." He pointed at the folder Nixon held.

Agent Nixon threw up his hands, "do either of you even know the contents of this?"

Both Agents just stared. Nixon shook his head. "Get out of my sight, the both of you. Now!" He looked over in my direction and shook his head.

"I think I now know why Washington wants you on a live case. I assume you heard all of that?" Nixon growled.

"Weres hear a lot. Sorry. May I see the report?" I took the folder from him and read what little information it contained. According to the veterinarian, both dogs tangled with a larger animal bigger than them. It tore out chunks of flesh, and teeth marks were found on both dogs' necks.

"It looks as though both dogs fought a larger animal. The bigger creature caught them by the neck and shook, breaking the neck on each," I explained to him.

"What is bigger than them?" Nixon asked me.

"A Were would be. Mass doesn't mean a thing when we the change is upon us," I informed him.

Nixon nodded as if in understanding. "Let's go check out the crime scenes, then. Maybe you can tell us what we are really hunting here."

Chapter Two

The first crime scene was a ranch-style house in what appeared to be a higher middle-class neighborhood. Yellow crime scene tape still surrounded the house, making it stand out like a sore thumb among the carefully manicured yards. It was the weekend, so many of the neighbors were watching as we pulled up in the driveway.

Agent Nixon climbed out of the SUV and motioned for me to follow him. We ducked under the tape and stepped up to the porch. The Agent waved to a dark colored sedan parked in front of the house.

Motioning with his chin he nodded toward the car. "It's a local police undercover unit. They have a theory that the unsub will return to the crime. Someone has been watching too much TV around here."

"Why let them keep doing it then?" I looked at the car. They stuck out in this neighborhood like a sore thumb.

"They have been guarding both the house and the scene, so why not? Their police chief won't listen to reason. We don't know the true situation according to him." The Agent climbed the steps and onto the porch. The door to the house was secured with a special police lock. Agent Nixon typed in a code and the lock released. At his touch, the door opened.

"As reported, the Smiths had four children. Greg Smith, the oldest, found them when he showed up as a surprise early in the morning. Local police units responded and found the parents and three children dead in their beds. Later inspection found a dog carcass in the backyard, leading them to believe it was the point of entry. We weren't called in until the second family was discovered." The lower level of the house was pristine except for evidence markers and signs that fingerprint teams had been through the area. A large oak staircase led to the upper levels. Holiday decorations draped the finials with bows and flowers.

"Our units failed to find any strange or non-familial fingerprints in this area. We have Agents investigating possible secondary family." We climbed the stairs to the second level.

"The son apparently thought to surprise his parents and entered their bedroom to find them slaughtered like sheep." We entered the first door on the left. A large king-sized bed dominated the room. Blood was everywhere. I stopped just inside the doorway and took a deep breath through my nose.

The killers scent was everywhere in the room. I could smell both his excitement and his sexual arousal. He'd gotten off on killing these people. I carefully stepped around Agent Nixon and circled the bed. The Were had stood here and watched them sleep before acting. He left pheromone trace everywhere not bothering to hide his presence at all.

I looked up to find my new boss looking at me. "He stood here and watched them for a time. He killed the man first and then the woman. He got off on it. There might be traces of that near the bed."

"What sort of Were is he?" Nixon asked me.

"He's a Wolf. They are the most predominate of all Weres. I can smell his anticipation and his arousal. The profile isn't complete at all. He's a sexual predator. Where are the children's rooms?"

Agent Nixon led me down the hall past the bathroom. I didn't need direction after that; the scent of blood was unmistakable. The door was slightly ajar and the carnal scent drifting out put my hackles on edge. I stepped inside and took a deep breath.

"Well?"

I shook my head. "He killed the boys first. Their terror permeates the room." I could see some signs of struggle, complete with evidence tags. "They must have heard the murders of their parents and were trying to escape. He killed them quickly so he could get the reaction he wanted from the girl. She was more terrified than the boys. He played with her."

"You mean he..." The Agent looked shocked.

"No. He didn't touch her physically. Have you ever watched a cat play with a mouse? He let her think she was getting away and then he killed her. This guy was very methodical. He touched almost nothing. Only another Were would have known he was here. Did you have any Magickal Support check out the crime scene?"

Agent Nixon was studying the floor and looked up quickly. "MS? No. We only have one of those guys on the payroll around here and he wasn't available. Do you think he would have helped?"

"Some Wizards can detect Weres. Or at least that is what my roommate at the Academy told me. It is an acquired skill, but they can do it, even the Russians," I explained to him.

"Who was your roommate?" Nixon asked.

"Agatha Blackmore. She's the first Official Federal Witch the FBI has ever recruited. Magical Crimes has her out west at the moment," I told him. Sniffing I checked out the closet and dressers just to be complete in my investigation.

"I heard there was a Witch at Quantico. Didn't she try to burn down the school?" He looked at me funny.

"Not exactly. Let's go out back. I need to check the yard. I'll tell you on the way." I looked at the room and shuddered. Those poor children didn't have a fighting chance. Agent Nixon followed me down the stairs. As we walked, I told him the crazy story.

"So wait a minute, a Director of the FBI was trying to kill her? Was he crazy?" Nixon had stopped and was staring at me.

"Maybe? They fired him for cause. If he was prosecuted over it is a mystery to me. The new Director of Quantico is very nice. She wasn't too pissed at some of Agatha's antics. Strange things just happen around her sometimes," I answered with a chuckle.

He shook his head at me. "It sounds to me like we all better watch out. You're trouble." He was smiling, so I guess he was kidding.

In back of the house was a nicely trimmed expansive backyard. A six-foot wooden fence ran the entire length of it. In the center was a small roped-off area with evidence markers. Much of the scent was gone due to it being outside, but it was there, too.

"The Smiths didn't have a dog, so whose is this? Did anyone canvas the neighborhood about a missing dog?"

Agent Nixon stared at the fence. "Not to my knowledge. We assumed it was theirs. The fence is pretty tall...seems unlikely that a dog could jump in...or out."

"You should have checked with a K9 unit. German Shepherds can jump six to eight feet. If this one wanted over he could have gotten over." I jumped up to the top of the fence and held on. Carefully I pulled myself up to a sitting position. From up here I could see three of the neighbors' yards. The one to the rear was a giant truck garden with greenhouses and solar panels. I doubted they had animals. Dogs could tear up a garden. The house to my right had a similar yard, complete with dog house. I didn't hear any barking. Most dogs go crazy when a Were is near, especially us Cats. I stood up on the top of the fence and peered over into the left-hand yard. It also had a dog house, but I could faintly hear barking. Sensing Agent Nixon's distress, I stepped backwards off the fence and flipped into a standing position.

The Agent's eyes were large as he gasped. "How did you just do that?"

"WereCat, remember? We are very agile. The yard behind us

doesn't look to have animals, but the ones on either side of us have dog houses. You're the boss, which one first?"

The house on the left was not our culprit, but they sent us in the proper direction. They raised Corgis and the three in the house were going crazy by the time we finished interviewing the homeowner.

"They sure didn't like you very much!" Nixon stated.

I smiled. "Yeah, well, regular animals aren't fond of Weres. In early human history they were kept in the house to detect us. I personally love dogs. My dad has two. If they are raised in the house as pups they don't react so badly around us. At least not normally."

"I see that." We traipsed across the Smith's yard to the house on the right. According to the Corgi owner, these folks had a 'big' dog.

Agent Nixon rang the doorbell and we waited for a response. Unlike the previous house, there wasn't a cavalcade of barking.

"Yes, can I help you?" We could hear the voice from a small speaker next to the door.

"Ma'am, I'm Agent Nixon with the FBI. Can we talk to you about the Smiths next door?"

"One moment, young man." I could hear steps approaching as someone came down the stairs and into what sounded like a hallway.

The door opened about an inch. "What can I do for you, young people?" The voice belonged to an older gray-haired woman.

"We wanted to ask you about the Smiths next door. Did they have a dog?" Nixon asked.

"Those poor dears! It's so sad about them." She stared at Nixon for a moment. "I'm sorry, you asked about something, didn't you?"

"Yes, Ma'am. Did they have a dog?" He asked again.

"A dog? No Agent Nixon, was it? Mrs. Smith was allergic to them. The little ones would come over here and play with Hercules all the time." She had a sad look on her face.

I spoke to her. "Ma'am, who is Hercules?"

"He's my dog. I've been calling for him, but he seems to have run off again." A tear ran down her face. This was going to break her heart.

"Is Hercules a German Shepherd?" I asked her.

"Why yes he is. How did you know? Have you seen him?" She had a slight smile on her face.

"I'm so sorry Ma'am. Hercules was killed protecting the Smith children from their attacker. We found him in their backyard," I told her.

"What! Poor Hercules." She started to cry. I nudged the door open and gave her a big hug. I held the crying woman for a few moments.

She pulled away and looked ashamed. "I'm sorry about that. He has been my constant companion for many years. He tried to save the children?"

I glanced at Agent Nixon. "Yes, Ma'am. He must have sensed the attacker and jumped the fence. We found his body in the backyard, so he was not successful. The FBI has taken care of his remains, along with local Animal control. I can give you their number if you like."

"No need for that, dear. Thank you, both of you." She closed the door with a sob. I heard footsteps go down the hall.

"Why did you do that, Moore? That dog wasn't trying to save the children." Nixon asked me.

"It may have been. Animals are more intelligent than many give them credit for. Besides, it was the dog that gave us a new lead in the case. And she needed something to hold on to. He was her friend too," I told him.

He nodded his head. "OK, that I can see. Do you need to see the other crime scene, too?"

"I don't think so. The dog was the biggest question I had. We now know we are looking for a WereWolf. I did think of a question for the other neighbor, though," I told him.

"What was that?" We were walking back to our car.

"Have there been other times the dogs went crazy? Maybe the choice of victims wasn't random at all. He might have cased the place out first," I explained.

Agent Nixon stopped and stared at me. "Sounds like we need to canvas the neighborhood. I think we have some Agents that can do that task."

I smiled at him knowingly. Too bad for them!

An hour later at the office we found our victims.

"I don't understand. You want me to knock on doors? Can't we use the pool for that? Why do I have to do it?" Agent Ramirez had a look of shock upon her face.

"You, Jones, and Cavelli dropped the ball on this one by missing the dog connection. We need to get back in the game here. Find another connection and find it now. Go!" He pointed to the door. The three Agents moped out and went to work.

"I was a little pissed when I was told to assign you to our group, Agent Moore, but you are pretty sharp. Maybe we can catch this guy, after all," Nixon explained to me.

I smiled at his praise. "You can call me Catherine or Cat if you like. I think we should send the Agents in the pool out to some of the other neighborhoods, too. This guy may be cruising, looking for another house. They should ask about strangers and animal behavior. We don't want a Witch hunt. Lots of innocent Weres in the area."

"There are?" He looked surprised.

"Of course there are. We aren't restricted to the reservations anymore. That was abolished in 1957. Many of my people stay there because it's the only life they remember. My father has a lodge and hunting club in Kentucky. He's very successful at it. Weres are just people, Agent Nixon. There are bad seeds among us as much as there are among humans." I pointed out.

"Like I said before. Welcome to the team, Agent Moore."

THE CANVAS DONE by the team turned up a few instances of dogs and cats going crazy when someone was around. One of the town's postal carriers was a WereFox, so I had to cross those on his route off the map. Agents were sent to ask Fox if he'd smelled any strangers.

The pool Agents turned up over thirty instances of erratic animal misbehavior in their neighborhoods. A pattern was starting to emerge. We were looking for a lawn service or yard worker. It was the only reason for a rogue to be in some of those neighborhoods and not be noticed as a stranger. Unfortunately, there were over thirty services in the area. We still had lots of work to do.

Chapter Three

No one realizes how invasive the yard work people can be. They cut your grass and trim your hedges. Some services clean the pool and wash the house exterior. They see you when you are sleeping and they know when you are gone. I'd heard of a case in Florida of a team of mowers robbing houses. They'd pull up start to mow and break into the house at the same time. Police caught them when neighbors wondered why the lawn-obsessed-neighbor was paying someone to cut his yard. In town there where were actually more than thirty lawn services, not counting the freelancers, working the neighborhoods.

"Did you realize how big a project this was going to be?" Agent Nixon stared at the map of the neighborhood.

"Not really. I didn't take into consideration the other areas." I pointed at the map and all the pins. "Most of the services stay to a certain area. It's the freelancers that are the problem. We have narrowed it down to five specific ones."

"You have already? Which five?" The Agent's eyes widened.

I nodded. "The pool was extremely helpful. The information they compiled is what will solve this one. The five independents are Bob's Mow and Blow, Men with Mowers, Grass King, Smith's All-in-One, and Any Job, Any Price."

"Some of those sound like higher quality services." Agent Nixon was watching me.

"They do, which is why this is so confusing. According to the services we interviewed, the freelancers don't play fair. The services get together once a year and map out what areas they are going to work from. They're planning to actually organize and form a mowers' union around here because of them. The freelancers pirate their supposed territories and poach customers. Those are their words, not mine sir."

Nixon nodded. "So one of the poachers is our man. Wolf. Whatever he is."

I motioned to the white board on the wall. "Right. The services turned over their employment and territory maps to us. We haven't found any known Weres among them. It has to be the freelancers."

"Do we have eyes on them yet?" Nixon asked.

"I have Agents watching their business addresses and others patrolling the neighborhood. The local LEOs are starting to catch on, however. You should expect a visit before long," I explained.

Agent Nixon had moved to the window. "I think that visit is going to happen in a minute or two, actually. Come on. I want you in on this." He motioned to me as he left the room. "Cover that map, first. Let's not help them out too much. I don't want them stumbling all over my investigation right now."

I threw a sheet over the pin-covered map and carefully closed the door. Our base of operations was an old office complex that the FBI leased from the city. The locals still treated it as their own property, regardless of our lease. Police Chief Melvin Lleras was a short chunky bald man with a loud voice. He was demonstrating its use to Agent Ramirez at the reception desk.

"I want to speak to whoever is in charge here! You people are all over the neighborhoods and are questioning everyone. You suspect somebody, and I want to know who! Right freaking now!"

"Calm down, Chief. SAIC Nixon is still in charge and will be here in a moment. Why don't you sit right here next to me and cool off? I know it's super hot out there."

"Hot! It's like sixty-five degrees. Stop using your womanly wiles on me, Agent Ramirez. What are you an Agent of, anyway? Prostitution?" He was staring at Ramirez as she blinked her eyes and thrust her chest at him.

"Chief Lleras, nice to see you again. What can the FBI do for you today?" Agent Nixon stepped out with his hand extended.

"You can include me in my own damn case, that is what you can do! I know it's a serial killer. Half the country knows that already. What I want to know is what you've discovered?" The Chief bellowed.

"Chief Lleras, you know we don't discuss open cases with anyone," Nixon replied to him.

"I'm the one that invited you in to MY case! What is going on?" The little bald man's face was getting redder and redder. He was starting to look like a fat matchstick.

Agent Nixon glanced at me and I smiled. Sighing heavily, he looked back at the fuming man. "We rechecked the crime scenes and now believe it was a rogue Were who was responsible for the murders. The dead dogs were the key."

"A Were? Like a WereWolf? How did you detect that?" The Chief sat heavily into one of the chairs and looked keenly at us. Agent Nixon leaned back on the front counter.

"As you may know, we have Weres on the FBI's payroll. According to the one we used, the Unsub is a male Wolf. At the first scene, we found a dead dog in the back yard. The victims didn't own a dog. It was a neighbor dog that jumped the fence and attacked the wolf. The veterinarian discovered teeth marks on both dogs."

"So the sharp knife we have been looking for is a claw?" The Chief was now calm and focused. He didn't seem to be the bumbler that Nixon had spoken about.

"Yes. It is. He killed the parents then the children and didn't leave any human trace. We found animal hair, but originally thought it belonged to the dogs. We also believe it wasn't random. The Smiths were specifically targeted," Nixon started to explain.

"So why are your people ripping my town apart? I'm going to find out sooner or later, so how about you tell me now. I know more about my town than you do; we can help." The Chief was staring at Agent Nixon.

I grabbed Agent Nixon's arm and pulled him off to one side. "I know you want to keep this in house, but look how that has worked so far. We know it's one of those five freelancers, but maybe he knows the players better than we do since it's his town?"

Agent Nixon scratched his ear for a moment and stared at me. Shaking his head, he sighed. "Agent Moore, Cat, you know regs as well as I do. We aren't supposed to involve the locals in our investigations unless necessary."

"I know that, but this is now a case for Magical Crimes if it involves a Were. Do you want to wait for them to show up? My friend Agatha is helping them out. I think they are in the Las Vegas area right now. I'm sure the case will wait for them to get here." I told him. We'd have another dead body by then though.

"That's dirty pool, Cat. Fine. We will tell the locals. Do not inform them of your status. I want that as an ace in the hole if we have to take on the Were in his other form. Will he respect your Alpha status? Or will he fight you?" Nixon asked me.

I really wasn't sure about that. The Wolves at the Academy were afraid of me, but only after they saw my other form. "I'm not sure. He will after I shift, but I don't know at this moment."

"OK then. Remember, don't disclose that to the Chief." We both turned back to the local officer.

"Chief Lleras, this is Agent Catherine Moore. She will fill you in. Agent?" He stepped back from me.

"Sir, normal animals are not fond of the Were. Most natural animals aren't, either. We were able to ascertain that the neighborhood dogs reacted violently when certain people were around. Our Agents canvased the surrounding four neighborhoods." I pulled the sheet off the map-board.

The Chief stepped closer to the map. "Our data shows that the overwhelming majority of animal reactions happen in the vicinity of local lawn services. Your community has over thirty of them. We've ruled out the professional ones, and are concentrating on the free-lancers. Of that group, we have narrowed it down to five." I handed him the list.

He glanced at the list and smiled. "My cousin Jimmy runs one of the more professional groups, so I know a bit about this stuff. I've heard him bitching about all the poachers on his business."

"Really? Which one does he run?" I looked at the Chief. Maybe he really could help us out.

"It's called Kensington Lawn and Pool, but everyone around here calls it Jimmy's Septic service. Cutting lawns is only a side job for my cousin. If you went by his shop you would understand. There is a big sign out front that says 'Septic Systems Drained and Pools Filled. Not Same truck.' I keep trying to get him to change it, but he says it's an attention grabber. Now, the ones on this list are interesting. Most of these guys are second jobbers. Bob works out at the airport and picks up work on the side. The same goes for the Men with Mowers. They're city workers who cut a little on the side. Grass King is James Stevenson."

"Stevenson. Why does that name seem familiar to me?" Agent Nixon started digging through his files.

Laughing, the local officer leaned back in the chair he sat in. "Save your search, Agent. He sounds familiar because he rented you the building. He's your landlord. Our culprit is either Smith or that last one. I don't know either of those outfits. There have been some reports of shady repairs and roofing scams around here lately. I'll check with my officers and see what I can dig up. You say dogs don't like Weres?"

"Yes, Chief. They don't," I informed him.

"Hmm. Well I'll have my boys bring a hunting dog with them on patrol from now on. We might catch this guy yet," the Chief told me.

"Chief, please tell them not to shoot the suspect. We don't want to harm an innocent Were, here!" This man worried me a bit.

"Little lady, we know our own out here. There are a few lone wolves out here as well as a very nice family of WereBeavers over near the river. We can handle it." He stood and tipped his hat at me as he sauntered away.

"I hope we don't have every yahoo with a gun out there now. That is all we need." Agent Nixon watched the Chief drive off from the window.

"He knew about the Weres in town which is a plus. I think his efforts will herd the unsub towards us." I traced the highway on the map. "If we set up a few road blocks or safety inspections here, here, and here, we will bottleneck him. He will have to take either this road or that one to get out of town in a hurry." I pointed to roads that looked like goat trails on the map.

"What if he goes Wolf and tries cross-country?" Agent Nixon stared at the map.

"Most rogues or loners can't hold their wolf form for more than an hour normally. We need the social bonds we form to help us control our second nature. It would take longer than that to cross this stretch of ground. See the drainage ditch here and the large rocks? Those would suck as a Wolf to cross. No, he will try one of the roads."

Agent Nixon smiled as he watched me. "What?" I asked. "Is there a bug on me or something?"

"No, Agent Moore. Nothing like that. I'm impressed. Usually the caliber of Agents we get are not anything like you. They sit in the pool and try to learn real world things until we need them. You are different, and it's refreshing."

"Oh. Was Ramirez a pool Agent?" I asked.

"I think you already know the answer to that one, Cat. Now let's get some road blocks set up and call the Chief back. He'll be pissed but he already hates us."

As Agent Nixon predicted, word spread rather quickly about

our suspects, and many people tried to leave town early. Even a few local Weres left, suspecting a witch hunt.

"No, Mrs. Blacktail. We don't suspect you or your family. This is just routine. I know you've heard about the killer in town. We are pretty sure he's a Wolf, not a Beaver," I explained to her.

At the word Wolf, the WereBeaver's body became rigid for a moment and a sharp musk filled the interrogation van. "Calm yourself ma'am. He's not here. I promise." I tried exerting some of the Alpha awareness I have. She calmed down, but I couldn't tell if it was me who caused it to happen.

Speaking slowly I started talking. "Can you tell me if you or your family have seen any Rogue activity around town? Police Chief Lleras has already told us about your family, so don't worry about that."

The WereBeaver looked at me and gave me a long sniff. She shuddered slightly and looked me in the eye. "You must be a strong Alpha, to affect other species. That is a first for me, to be influenced by a predator. Be careful of that power, young lady. It can be seductive. In answer to your question, we haven't. There are a couple of lone Wolves in town. Both are Omegas and are frightened half to death that their Packs will find them or someone will dominate them. They wouldn't do something like this. If you must talk to them, they run the computer repair shop on Main. I will tell my family not to run."

Agent Nixon gave me a raised eyebrow look as the older lady got back into her car and left. "Weres don't normally attack other Weres, but there is some history of it. Many of us are predators. We have the same issues natural predators have." I smiled at him.

"So I should send a regular Agent to talk to the Omegas? What is an Omega?" Nixon asked.

"Yes. Send another of the team. Tell them to be gentle. Omegas are subs. Think of them as the most dominated person in a group of Alpha personalities. They usually bow to the wishes of everyone in the Pack. In my father's Pack, the Omega is the healer and the peacekeeper. I can't imagine what would cause two of them to leave. Since we are busy at the moment, I'll leave that mystery to you for now." I explained.

"That's probably a good idea." He turned back to his radio and sent a few commands to check out the computer shop.

The sound of a squeal of tires and a police siren made law enforcement personnel snap their heads up and look around. A green Chevy truck with ladders and tools hanging off of it came around the corner at a high rate of speed. Hot on its tail was one of the local police cars. We had tire-shredders deployed and the truck ran over three of them. In a swirl of smoke and burning rubber, the green truck crashed into one of the cars being used as a roadblock. Agents rushed forward, heedless of danger, and pulled open the door.

"On the ground! Get on the ground now!" Black acrid smoke began to pour from beneath the hood of the truck. The man behind the wheel was coughing and hacking from the smoke. I could smell oil and gas as it leaked to the ground.

"Get him out of the truck! It's going to catch fire!" I yelled at the other Agents, but they didn't hear me. Orange and red flames began to lick out and consume the front of the vehicle. One brave Agent burst from cover and grabbed the driver pulling him from the truck. Cries of "Get on the ground!" began again.

Agents placed handcuffs on the man as he lay there. The truck was now fully engulfed, and the fire was spreading to the car it had impacted. Sirens in the distance heralded the fire department.

"Well, that was easy. The Chief just reported they tried to ask him some questions and he attacked the office and ran for it. So much for being dangerous." Agent Nixon had a big smile on his face. I wasn't so sure about that.

"Are they using the Were-proof cuffs on him?" I asked him.

"Should we be? I mean, he's subdued." Nixon looked to his Agents and the suspect.

There was a scream and a loud roar as the suspect got to his feet and broke out of the cuffs. Hair began to appear on his face and arms.

"Damn it! Make sure nobody shoots me." I began stripping off my suit pants and jacket. The Wolf was now completely changed and was attacking the Agents. Gunshots could be heard as the panicking Agents fired wildly.

"Cat, what are you doing! Now is not the time for...Oh my God!" He fell backward as my other form made her presence known with a very loud roar.

The Wolf's head came up with a growl as he sensed a challenger. He bared his teeth and looked around the smoke-filled area. Gunshots still sounded, and he flinched as a bullet struck his flank. The Agents had disregarded my instructions and weren't using the silver bullets the FBI issued. Good for him and good for me. My Cat screamed her challenge and leaped over the police car with ease.

My form was easily three times the size of his. I was what the Packs called a throwback. Every generation, there was maybe one born worldwide. I was a Sabertooth tiger in my other form, the rarest of the rare.

The Wolf growled at me and looked for a way out. I began to pace in front of the cars and crouched for a leap. It lunged forward trying to bite my flank. Lashing out with my four-inch razor sharp claws I severed the front leg from his body. With a hiss and a growl, my Cat closed in for the kill. When Weres change, we become two consciousnesses in one body. Usually the most primal is the dominate one. With Alphas, we have the option to control our other form and retain our intellect and thought. Knowing the need to keep him alive, I reigned her in and pulled back from the Wolf.

The rogue lay on the ground and slowly began to change back to human. The Agents were freaking out and pointing guns at the both of us. Shifting to my warrior form, freaking the Agents out even more, I grabbed the severed limb and jammed it up against the shifting Wolf's wound. His limb reattached itself as he shifted back to human.

"Puut theee Weerre cufffs on himm," I growled at the others.

I stood guard until finally someone did as I asked. Growling I stepped around the car and scooped up my clothing. There was a wooded area nearby where I could change.

Firefighters were putting out the vehicle fires, adding steam to the black smoke as I out of the woods, I found Agent Nixon waiting for me beside one of the patrol cars.

"That wasn't in your file." He looked me up and down, perhaps seeing me for the first time.

"Were forms usually aren't. How is the suspect?" I asked.

"Recovering. I was surprised the arm took. Is that normal for your people?" He asked.

Arching my eyebrow, I gave the SAIC a look. "It can be. He would have regrown it in a few weeks, but I thought you would like him in one piece for the interrogation. Please tell me you used the proper cuffs this time?"

"We did. He's in a reinforced cell that the locals have. Guards with silver ammo are watching him." I spotted my shoes on the ground and picked them up.

"It seems they are as incompetent as we thought then," I said. "He smells like the one we want. Is he?"

"He is. We searched the place he was living and found evidence he was in the homes. DNA will be the final nail in his coffin, but we're pretty sure he's our guy. Good work, Agent Moore." Agent Nixon held out a hand to me.

Shaking it I thanked him.

There wouldn't be any more pool time for me. They were all frightened of me now, anyway.

"That was something of a surprise, young lady. I guess size doesn't matter for your folk?" Chief Lleras smiled at me when I entered his station to view the suspect.

I snorted, "not so much. May I see the suspect?"

"Sure thing. I spoke to Mrs. Blacktail. She told me you were more than you seemed to be." The Chief seemed very sure of himself and was less country sounding.

"She seemed like one tough lady. Is she OK?" I asked.

The Chief nodded. "One of her kids works for me around the farm. He says she's fine. Very good work, miss. Very good. If the FBI doesn't work out, you come talk to me, you hear?"

"My dad said the same thing, but thanks. It's nice to have options." He led me through a few doors into a what looked like the older part of the building.

"This is the oldest jail in the state. We kept the original cells just in case we needed to lock up a Were. One of the first reservations was in our county. It's gone now. Better to be prepared, don't you think?" The Chief replied as he say my look of surprise.

This man was way more wily than Nixon gave him credit for. All they lacked was a Were on force around here. "Yes, Sir."

The last cell contained the Wolf I had fought. He was shackled to the wall.

"So do you wish to say anything? I assume you have been read your rights?" The Chief nodded to me. There were cameras in place, so everything was recorded.

"I've got nothing to say to your kind, Cat! Your kind is worse than these inferior mundies!" The Wolf rogue yelled. He rattled the chains trying to pull himself loose.

"OK. Your choice." I followed the Chief out of the cell area.

"So did he say anything worthwhile?" Agent Nixon sat in the Chief's office.

"No, Sir. What happens to him now?" I asked.

"Now? The State Attorney and the Federal Attorney get to fight it out on pay-per-view. That's what happens now." Police Chief Lleras stated with a smile.

"It's in discussion. Don't worry, someone will try him for murder." Nixon stood and shook Lleras's hand. "Time for us to go. We have paperwork to fill out and work to do."

As we exited the building, I smiled. I caught the bad guy! Wait until I tell Agatha all about it. Maybe I was ready to do this job after all. Time to learn whatever I could to make my future job easier.

AUTHOR NOTE

Surprise! My wife gets all the credit for this one. It was her idea to put this collection out before the release of The Federal Witch Book 3, so everyone can get caught up. That book is still being written but will drop with luck by the end of January 2017. So real soon. I have more than 5 books planned for this series for the next year, as well as my Sci - Fi books and others.

2016 was a year of trials and tribulations for me as an author. I started out with literally nothing and now have over 23 books in publication.

WHAT'S THE NEXT BOOK IN THE SERIES?

The room was dark. So dark I couldn't even see my own hands. Water dripped from the walls. Each drop making a plopping noise as it echoed somewhere in the darkness. The very air was like blanket of moisture encompassing my entire being. "Where am I?"

My voice echoed off into the distance. The sound of it made me dizzy. Where? This time I said it almost as a prayer. My last thoughts were of the new assignment and the possible advantage that Fergus would bring us. A talking Unicorn would be a boon to anyone investigating the species. That is of course if he would cooperate in the first place. None of that mattered though. I needed to know what this place was and how I got here. Mumbling a short cantrip spell I cast a light spell into being. Looking down I almost screamed!

Bones! As far as the light reached the entire floor of the cave was covered in bones. Pools of water lay here and there. My light spell floated above me like a glowing ball. Mentally I pushed it out farther to see if a path lay through the horror. Flickering shadows moved down the walls as the ball moved. Now that I could see the bones I began to notice the smell. A sense of decay filled the air. I tried to tell myself it was all in my mind.The ball of light bobbed and weaved through the cave I found myself in. How did I get here and where is the rest of my team? A flash of something caught my eye as my light reached the far edge.

Navigating through the darkness constantly stepping over bones I felt like a female version of Theseus. With luck there wouldn't be a Minotaur at the end of my journey. I was lost in a cave of horror without a solid clue of how I got here. Such is my life.

Gold and silver covered the altar. What I saw flashing was gem encrusted goblets and priceless statues of the Gods as well as trappings of the modern world. Cell phones older than me as well as what appeared to be my own lay scattered on the floor. Swords and axes lay piled amongst rifles and handguns. This was an monument to war and destruction. I might not worship Mars but I could see his handy work. Peering closer I looked at the God statues themselves. Worn from centuries of handling the features were hard to see. I was mistaken. Mars and Odin were never here. This massacre was a tribute to the God of chaos and war. All of this belonged to Set!

"Why am I here?" Once again the cave echoed my words.

"Who says you are?"

Spinning around I saw several black clad figures standing in the distance. A faint green glow clung to them like it was painted on them.

"What?" I felt my eyes widen as the figure in the fronts eyes began to glow the same sickly green.

"This place is ours. It always has been and always will be. To get here you must joint the order and sacrifice to Set and only then will you earn the honor of a chance to join us." The words dripped from the mouth of the ancient woman standing in front of me.

"Set." My eyes narrowed in concentration.The word was echoed throughout the cavern, unlike the ancient woman's words.

The woman stepped out of the shadows followed by a half dozen others. Each drew sacrificial daggers and held them low in tight grips. My ball of light made the blades shine with unholy light. "What say you child of light? Will you join us and fulfill the potential that your family saw in you years ago or will you die? This is your moment of truth. I swear by Set and our Goddess that we will either possess you or kill you!" The women continued to advance toward me faster now.

Mumbling, I cast a freeze spell followed by a several fireballs. None of what I threw at them worked. They moved closer and closer to me. Starting to panic I backed up. Not watching where I was walking my feet hid one of the skeletons causing me to loose my balance and fall backwards. One minute I was backing away the next I was on my ass with a ribcage locked firmly around my ankle. Shaking my leg like a cat with a rubber band I tried to stand. Hearing laughter I looked up.

"So the mighty fall. Get up little Witch. It's not like you have anywhere to go." The green-eyed woman waved her hand and torches suddenly lit along the walls of the cave.

Still struggling I kicked the old bones off and forced myself up. The walls all around me were not faintly lit. There were no exits.

"Submit to us Agatha Blackmore. We offer training and power the likes of which this world has never seen."

Finding my voice at last I yelled my response. "I submit to no one. Not you or your God of chaos. My choices are my own. You may attack me now but you will never break those that stand against you."

"Pretty words. But we know different don't we, young Witch. We know of the doubt and hurt that infests your heart. You will belong to us one day. Fate is fickle that way." She woman raised her arm, tossing the knife she held straight at my head.

Using skill I didn't know I had I managed to catch the blade. Shocked I stared at it in surprise. All those sessions with Cat and Chuck seemed to have paid off finally.

"Impressive. Try stopping this one." A green glowing ball of flames headed straight at me.

Screaming I covered my head with my hands. I could feel the heat of the flames as the fireball touched my skin and then nothing.

OTHER BOOKS BY TS PAUL

I welcome comments and questions on my blog. Follow me on Facebook or visit my Amazon author page. I have an author page with BookBub too.

I'm excited, are you?

The Federal Witch

Born a Witch Drafted by the FBI! - Now Available in Audio!

Conjuring Quantico - Now Available in Audio!

Magical Probi - Now Available in Audio!

Special Agent in Charge - Now Available in Audio!

Witness Enchantment

Night of the Unicorn

Invisible Elder

Blood on the Moon

Child of Darkness

A Draft of Dragons

Cat's Night Out, Tails from the Federal Witch - Audio Available

Serpent Con

Darkness Revealed

Unicorns Are Short

The Standard of Honor

Shade of Honor

Coven Codex

A Confluence of Covens -TBD

Conflict of Commitments -TBD

Standard of Honor -TBD

Familiar Magic

Familiar Shadows

Familiar Trials - Fledgling

Familiar Travels

The Wild Hunt

Witching Hour

The Wild Hunt

Furious Magic

The Mongo Files

The Case of the Jamaican Karma -TBD

The Case of the Lazy Magnolia - TBD

The Case of the Rugrat Exorcist -TBD

Monster Hunter

Jack Dalton Book 1

Jack Dalton Book 2

Jack Dalton Book 3

Jack Dalton Book 4

Jack Dalton Book 5

Jack Dalton Book 6

Magical Division Origins

Jack Dalton, Monster Hunter Box Set (1-3)

Jack Dalton, Monster Hunter Box Set (4-6)

Cookbooks From the Federal Witch Universe

Marcella's Garden Cookbook

Fergus Favorites Cookbook

Marcella's Summer Bounty Cookbook

Marcella's Autumn Harvest

Eat and Read Cookbooks

Badger Hole Bar Food Cookbook

Taking it on the Road

Athena Lee Chronicles

The Forgotten Engineer

Engineering Murder

Ghost Ships of Terra

Revolutionary

Insurrection

Imperial Subversion

The Martian Inheritance - Audio Now Available

Infiltration

Prelude to War

War to the Knife

Ghosts of Noodlemass Past

Athena Lee Universe

Shades of Learning

Space Cadets - Coming Soon

Smuggle Life

Double Cross

Politics Equals Death

Cut and Run

A Grand Affair

Short Story Collections

Wilson's War

A Colony of CATTs

Unicorns are Short

Borscht is Boring

Box Sets

The Federal Witch: The Collected Works, Book 1

Chronicles of Athena Lee Book 1-3

Chronicles of Athena Lee Book 4-6

Chronicles of Athena Lee Book 7-9 plus the prequel

Athena Lee Chronicles (10 Book Series)

Standalone or tie-ins

The Tide: The Multiverse Wave

The Lost Pilot

Uncommon Life

Dead in Space

Kutherian Gambit

Alpha Class. The Etheric Academy book 1

Alpha Class - Engineering. The Etheric Academy Book 2

The Etheric Academy (2 Book Series)

Holiday Tales

Watch Where You Dig

Night of the Living Turkeys

Reindeer Don't Fly

Anthologies

Phoenix Galactic

Cupid's Bow

Mysterious Hearts

Journal with a View: July - August - September

Haunted Hearts

Snapshots of Life I

Prime Peek I

Silent Thanks

Non-Fiction

Get that Sh@t off your Cover!: The so-called Miracle Man speaks out

Study Guide and Timeline: The Athena Lee Chronicles